THE MARK OF EDAIN

Also by Pauline Chandler
Warrior Girl

'A terrific tale set in medieval France. When Mariane's parents are murdered, she's drawn to her strange cousin, Jehanne, who claims she gets signs from God. You'll be left breathless with pure excitement.'
Mizz magazine

'The healing revelation with which this novel ends is so unexpected and utterly right that it made me gulp.'
Kevin Crossley-Holland, writing in the *Guardian*

Viking Girl

'As she demonstrated in *Warrior Girl*, the author has a remarkable ability to conjure up detail and atmosphere from the past.' *Children's Bookseller*

'Chandler has created an atmospheric background with a curious blend of pagan and Christian rites and beliefs, of realism and the supernatural. There are plenty of exciting episodes, action and adventure.'
School Librarian

PAULINE CHANDLER

THE MARK OF EDAIN

OXFORD
UNIVERSITY PRESS

OXFORD
UNIVERSITY PRESS

Great Clarendon Street, Oxford OX2 6DP

Oxford University Press is a department of the University of Oxford.
It furthers the University's objective of excellence in research, scholarship,
and education by publishing worldwide in

Oxford   New York

Auckland   Cape Town   Dar es Salaam   Hong Kong   Karachi
Kuala Lumpur   Madrid   Melbourne   Mexico City   Nairobi
New Delhi   Shanghai   Taipei   Toronto

With offices in

Argentina   Austria   Brazil   Chile   Czech Republic   France   Greece
Guatemala   Hungary   Italy   Japan   Poland   Portugal   Singapore
South Korea   Switzerland   Thailand   Turkey   Ukraine   Vietnam

Oxford is a registered trade mark of Oxford University Press
in the UK and in certain other countries

British Library Cataloguing in Publication Data

Data available

ISBN: 978-0-19-272089-4

3 5 7 9 10 8 6 4 2

Printed in Great Britain by CPI Cox and Wyman, Reading, RG1 8EX

Paper used in the production of this book is a natural,
recyclable product made from wood grown in sustainable forests.
The manufacturing process conforms to the environmental
regulations of the country of origin.

For Phoenix

CONTENTS

ESCAPE

There was one small rabbit left in the pen, in the corner of the kitchen, next to the window. It sat quiet and still, but Aoife could see what it dreamed in its bright black eye: of a grassy bank, sun-warmed, and a spreading warren over the hillside; the rabbit dreamed of being free.

'Me too,' Aoife whispered. She pushed her fingers between the loosely plaited willow wands of the pen until she touched the rabbit's fur, and glanced out of the window, as she often did, at the road which led into the city. On the far side were gardens and a field full of green shoots: good eating for a little rabbit. A slaver's wagon creaked into view. From dawn to dusk the road was busy with traffic: traders, pilgrims, soldiers, travellers, all making their way to Rome. She could do nothing for the slaves, nothing for herself, chained by the fetters between her ankles. Perhaps she could help the rabbit.

When Quintus, the cook, wiped his hands on his bloodstained apron and went to speak to the grocer's boy at the door, Aoife reached into the pen.

'Hey!' Quintus barked. Startled, the rabbit squirmed in her hands, but Aoife managed to push it across the sill and out of the window. If it escaped the wagon wheels and the clutching hands of traders, it had a chance to be

1

free. Better the chance, than certain death in Quintus's kitchen.

The cook's hard fingers dug into her shoulder. Aoife steeled herself for the blow to come, but he stayed his hand when Madoc, her brother, appeared, shouting, from under the archway that led into the house.

'Tessius Maximus is dead!' he cried. 'Our master's dead. It's true! It's true!'

His face alight, he stumbled into the kitchen. 'Mistress Lucilla thinks he's been poisoned and she wants to see you at once, Quintus!' *Quintus—not Master Quintus*. Aoife glanced at the cook, but, for once, he ignored the slight. Blanched with shock, he threw off his apron, and pushed past Madoc into the house.

Madoc came to Aoife and held up a knife. 'This lay on the floor next to Tessius's bed! He has no use for it, but we do.'

Aoife stared at the weapon. Gold filigree, intricate, polished steel blade: a rich man's dagger. 'How did Tessius die?' she said, as Madoc bent to use the knife as a lever to break through her chains. 'Was he stabbed?' *Madoc Hothead*. She grabbed his shoulders and made him stand face to face with her.

'No. I don't know. I don't think so!' Madoc said. 'You don't think I *killed* him?'

Aoife shook her head and let him go. *Madoc Softheart*. 'You shouldn't have touched the knife! If they find you with it—'

Madoc shrugged and went on levering at the chain.

'When did you find him?' Aoife said. 'What time was it?'

She glanced at the shadow cast by the gnomon on the carved dial halfway up the wall above Quintus's bench.

'Less than a quarter ago.'

'Were you alone?'

'Yes.'

'Did you hear anything?'

'No! It was the same as it is every morning. There were visitors, as always, not that I saw them. I heard their voices from my cubby hole next door.'

'Raised voices? Was there a quarrel?'

'No!'

'Who was the last to leave?'

'I didn't see. Keep still. I was busy cleaning shoes and watching for Rosa bringing the eggs. Then I went to prepare Tessius's bath. You know the routine. He likes me to mix the oatmeal into the water. *Liked*. When I went into the room it was all silent. Usually he talks to me; he doesn't expect me to answer, just listen, but this morning he didn't say anything. That's when I noticed that he was still in bed. I drew the curtain aside and there he was—' Madoc looked up at her '—all puffed up and purple. It looked like death by poison to me,' he said, then bent again to his task. 'I called Menander straightaway, but he wouldn't come at first, said he was busy with the accounts. I was hoarse by the time he arrived. I wish you'd seen his face, when he saw old Tessius! He went to tell Mistress Lucilla, then she sent me to fetch Quintus. And I saw a chance to escape.'

Aoife shot a glance at the archway leading into the house.

'It's foolish to run away now!' she said, jerking her foot

3

out of his hands. 'You might as well confess to murder! Why did you pick up the knife? It was stupid!' She shivered and hugged herself. Killing your master meant death. So did attempting to escape, not only for them but for the others. Stiff and wide-eyed, her kitchen companions watched them in silence: Pontius, Decius, Doranda. Fatima and Lucius.

A crash. Angry voices. The old woman, Fatima, stared at the corridor into the house, but Aoife could see that the noise came from the road. A wagon had overturned. No one looked at the villa, no one approached, no soldiers with swords drawn. Tessius's death was still a secret.

Decius stared at the vegetable knife he was holding, as if he had never seen it properly before, then began hacking at his fetters. The others followed his example. Pontius turned to free Fatima.

The shadow of the gnomon crept through the next quarter as the slaves worked on their chains: their luck held, no one came from the house.

The iron chinked as it dropped from Aoife's ankles. Four years she had worn it, day and night. She rubbed the scars; her legs felt loose and shaky, but she must move. Madoc was already climbing out of the window.

'The gods be with you,' he said to the others, as he left.

Fatima opened the back door that led into the orchard, then to the ploughed field and, beyond that, to the marsh, where you could disappear without trace. Guiding the others outside, she nodded to Aoife. *Be safe.*

Aoife jumped from the sill. Crouched next to Madoc, behind a dense laurel bush, she peered out at the garden path.

'Where do we go? Where do we head for?' Aoife said, shivering. The bright sun did not warm her.

'Sh!' Madoc pointed to a dark figure, coming in through the gate. 'It's the doctor,' he whispered. 'Lucilla must have sent for him. Wait until he goes into the villa, then we'll head for the road.'

The man in his dark scholar's gown went into the house, followed by his retinue of assistants, carrying bags and boxes and a live cockerel. Fearful cries came from the house.

Aoife and Madoc ran to the road.

'Wait—' Aoife said, darting back. She dug at a little patch of herbs near the portico, at the foot of the statue of Flora; her own patch of the garden, given to her by Master Tessius after she had cured him of a fever.

'Aoife! We have to leave—now!' Madoc called, running back to her.

'Not without this,' Aoife muttered, shaking soil from a small leather pouch. The door to the villa opened. Madoc shoved her behind the statue.

'Should have sent for me sooner,' the doctor called over his shoulder. He threw down the rag he was using to wipe his hands, and it landed in Aoife's patch. Mistress Lucilla, sobbing, wiped her red face with her shawl.

'I shall know more when I have examined the body,' the doctor said, keeping his distance. He straightened the folds of his cloak and said, with a look of distaste, 'Menander will see to the rites. Keep the cadaver as cool as you can.' Lucilla threw back her head, wailed, then snuffled into her robe. 'My men will collect it in the morning.'

'What about that powder?' Lucilla asked in a broken voice. 'My husband was always in pain after he took it. For all I know that was what killed him—your so-called remedy!'

She lumbered down the path, waving her crumpled shawl at the doctor.

'Nonsense, nonsense,' he said, increasing his pace. He hooked his finger at one of his servants who ran past him to open the gate. 'I shall know more tomorrow,' he called, before stepping into his litter.

Flicking aside the curtain, he craned his neck to look past the villa into the fields. 'Instead of making wild accusations, you should look to your household!' he said, pointing past the peach trees to where Fatima and the others, mere black dots at the far edge of the ploughed field, were escaping into the marsh.

'Aggghhhh! Stop them!' screamed Mistress Lucilla. 'Stop them! Menander! Menander!' She crushed the ends of her shawl in both fists and shook them at the heavens. 'Men-aaan-de-errrr!' When no one answered, with a last furious bleat she fled back into the villa.

As the doctor rode off in his litter, Madoc counted slowly to a hundred. 'That should do it,' he said. 'Ready?'

They ran down the path to the road. There, with a glance in both directions, Madoc murmured, 'We'll head for the Street of Silent Knives.'

THE STREET OF
SILENT KNIVES

Terror closed on Aoife like a fist, as she followed Madoc deep into the streets of Rome. She could not breathe properly. Her chest hurt. It was as if the shackles she had got rid of were now tightening invisibly around her whole body. She was free: she should feel exhilarated, but she was more afraid than she had ever been in her life.

Like a judge's gavel, the facts fell like blows on her mind: Tessius Maximus, their master and personal friend to the emperor, was dead, probably murdered; Madoc had found the body and run away; he had stolen a knife. Mistress Lucilla would search for them.

She saw spies on every corner, hard-faced men with dogs. Every shout made her jump as if stabbed, every look was from someone about to betray them to the soldiers or to the slave-catcher with his iron collars. She threw off her sandals to run faster.

As warm morning increased to noon heat, as they turned from one sleepy street into another, and they were not pursued, she allowed herself the faint hope that Madoc might be leading them to a place of safety, where they could rest, where she could think and plan their next step.

It seemed unlikely: their destination, *The Street of Silent*

Knives, sounded like a den of assassins. Yet, confident and strong, Madoc led the way. Did he have a plan?

Four years ago, when they had been brought to Rome, she was eleven and he only ten. Now he seemed the older one. He was taller, too, which was a good thing, wasn't it, for their father's heir?

She clutched the dusty pouch to her chest and ran her fingers down the outline of the bronze insignia inside. The badge belonged to Madoc; she had kept it for him. Perhaps it was time to hand it over.

'Living in the household of Tessius Maximus suited you,' she called. 'I hardly recognize you, now that I see you—' *free again?* She could not say the words, not yet. 'Out here—' she finished weakly, with a gesture to the street they were crossing.

Madoc hurried on through the maze of narrow alleys. 'I was well-fed, treated well, by and large, and trusted to come into the city on my own,' he replied, over his shoulder.

'Why didn't you stay at the villa then?'

'Need you ask? *I AM CELTOI!*'

'Shhh!' Aoife said, yet she was ashamed to silence his proud cry. *Celtoi. The tribes.* The name given to them by the Greeks.

'I shall never be Roman,' Madoc said. 'And I shall make Rome pay for the death of my father.' They stopped to catch breath.

'As shall I!' Aoife said. 'But first we must stay alive.' As Madoc ran on ahead, cold fear roiled inside her. 'Stop!' she called after him. 'Listen to me. We have to go back! We shouldn't have run away—'

'We can't go back! We were leaving today anyway—'
Madoc replied.

'What do you mean, we were leaving?'

Madoc stopped and turned to face her. 'We had to leave. Tessius was going to give us to the emperor.'

'*What?*'

'It's true. He was going to present us as a gift to the Emperor Claudius.'

Aoife walked slowly up to him. 'What are you talking about?'

'It's true. Tessius wanted to be a senator and he thought that Claudius would promote him, if he handed us over.'

'I don't understand. Tessius is dead—'

'That was nothing to do with me, I swear it. The plan was for us to leave the villa today, before the emperor got hold of us. Someone was supposed to come, before dawn, but they didn't come, and when I found Tessius dead, and the knife, well—the gods help those who help themselves, don't they? We're free, aren't we? No one's followed us and we're nearly there.'

'Where?'

'Look, Aoife, just follow me, right? Then you'll see for yourself.' He ran on.

'I don't understand,' she called. 'Why was Tessius handing us over now? We've lived under his roof for four years.'

'Claudius is about to lead an invasion of Britannia. We are kin of the British leader, *ergo*, valuable hostages. Think about it.'

Aoife looked up at the strip of blue sky between the

uneven line of tiled roofs, which leaned towards each other, almost touching, down the length of the long narrow street. Rome had waged war in Britannia for as long as she could remember. What was Madoc saying, that the emperor himself was going to Britannia, to fight Caradoc?

Lord Caradoc, her mother's brother, had led the most recent rebellion, so much she knew from kitchen gossip, and Caradoc was a mighty warrior. But the legions of Rome were so well trained, so efficient, that she hadn't dared to hope that his rebellion would succeed.

And, truthfully, if the emperor was about to face him, then Caradoc was already defeated, because Claudius would only go to Britannia if it was safe. The emperor would not risk himself in battle.

Caradoc. The Romans called him Caratacus. She swallowed the sourness of the Roman name from her mouth. 'Caradoc!' she called out loud.

'*What?*' said Madoc.

'Claudius will not bargain with the tribes!' she burst out. 'Why would he trouble himself? If he's going himself to Britannia, it means that the battle's over and Rome has won. He has no need of hostages. And now we're on the run, and if we're caught, we'll be killed—'Aoife was shocked motionless. *Tessius. Caradoc. Claudius.* She and Madoc were mere counters in a game played by others. The cold logic was terrifying. 'There must be no more *deaths*!' she cried. *Not in our family.* Long-buried ghosts stirred in her mind.

'None of it matters!' Madoc said. 'The Mother's with us—we're free! Claudius will not find us. And, best of all, we're going *home*!' He started to sing one of the old tunes, one that Anwyn, their nurse, had called the Home Song: *Where salt sea flows, Where wild herb grows, Where hawk flies free and curlew calls . . .*

'Madoc—' Aoife called, digging her nails into her palms. The song tempted fate. 'Mother grant us a time for singing.'

It was past noon. The sun beat down as vendors closed up their market stalls, which lined the alley, packing their goods away or covering them with white cloths.

Though no one paid them any attention, Aoife was still afraid. When the last servant girl closed the last shutter and gave them a curious stare, she pulled Madoc out of sight, under a portico in front of one of the houses. She sagged against the wall, catching breath, and rubbed her hand over her forehead. Running had tired her: she had not realized how hot it could be in the city. She had never left Tessius's villa to experience it. The only time she had left the kitchen was to visit the bath-house once a week, to use Mistress Lucilla's tepid bathwater to wash herself. And, every night, of course, to return to her cellar bed.

Now in the street, which was utterly silent, the ground shimmered with heat. Cicadas sang and a dog howled a wide yawn, then found a spot of shade and settled down to sleep in it.

'Where are we?' Aoife said, as Madoc went to the corner and peered into the next alley.

'Near the river,' was the reply.

The Tiber that led down to the sea. The sea that would take them home. Talk of home had disturbed her, had dislodged all those barriers she had so carefully placed, like poultices, over her memories. Now homesickness clouded her mind, as much her enemy as a Roman soldier.

Madoc signalled. 'We're almost there. Aoife, listen to me. We're going to find a man who will help us. He's not exactly your sort, but don't condemn him out of hand. He's a trader with his own fleet of ships, who will grant us safe passage back to Britannia.'

She pulled at Madoc, stopped him from moving on. 'Wait,' she said. She held out the pouch. 'Here, this is yours. You should have it, in case we're separated.'

Madoc opened the pouch. He slid out the piece of bronze, a thin rectangular plate, curved, with spikes at each corner. It was battered and bent from its true shape, with one of the corner spikes broken off, but the design on the front was smooth and unsullied. It showed the sigil of the tribe, of the Mother, Edain, the goddess of horses; the broad outlines of a horse's head, with slanting eyes made from polished green agate.

'The Mark of Edain,' Madoc breathed, and ran his fingers over the pattern. He reached up to the brand on his neck, then touched the same brand, grimy, but not faded, on the side of Aoife's neck, the mark of their tribe, scored into their flesh with a dark blue stain. Three horizontal lines, beneath it, marked their status, as son and daughter of the Druid Bevis, husband to the sister of Lord Caradoc, rebel leader of the Celts in Britannia.

They shared a smile. Madoc turned the bronze emblem over and over in his hands. 'How did you get hold of this?' he asked.

'I took it as we were leaving. No one saw me and no one bothered to search me on the boat. When we got to

Tessius's house, I pretended to be sick—do you remember?—and I shoved it under that bush. Later I dug the hole deeper and made a proper hiding place.'

Madoc put the badge back into the pouch, then shoved it into his belt. 'One day I shall take my father's place, at the head of the tribe.'

A familiar sound made Aoife stiffen. The sound of marching. At the far end of the alley, she caught the glint of a metal helmet.

'Soldiers!' she hissed.

She darted after Madoc, to the next turning, then hid behind a large bush in a pot on the corner as the commander shouted an order and the soldiers began their search of the street. Creeping backwards, his eyes on the guards, Madoc pulled her into the next alley. He looked at the houses. 'This is it! The Street of Silent Knives!'

Aoife scanned the line of tall narrow dwellings that faced each other in lines of identical facades, under a threatening gloom which hung over the alley like trailing smoke.

Barked orders disturbed the silence. They sped on towards the last few houses at the far end of the street, where there was a junction and daylight shining down on a wide road, and a glimpse of the river.

'It's one of these—' Madoc hesitated. They fell into the shadows as the soldiers turned into the alley. The commander hammered on a door.

'Slaves of Tessius Maximus! Come out now!' He stood back, shading his eyes, to stare up at the roof.

Madoc peered out. 'The emperor's men. He will search all Rome for us—'

Aoife felt light and unsteady. 'Where's this house?'

'It has ironwork shutters, with pictures of animals, bears, on either side of the front windows. Bears, yes.'

As the soldiers moved to the next dwelling, Aoife and Madoc scrambled under the pillared entrance to a five storey house, set back between the last two dwellings on the street. It looked derelict. A shower of plaster dust fell over them, as Madoc tapped at the door.

Aoife scanned the shutters. The soldiers moved again, then halted, as their commander knocked at another door. They stood to attention, searching every nook, every shadow, with their eyes. One man turned to look down the alley. He seemed to stare straight at Aoife. Then someone came out of the house and the soldier joined the others, pushing past the man to search inside.

Madoc pointed to the closed shutters, obscured by a dead vine with twiggy tendrils. 'Bears!' Aoife looked at the shutters: if you half closed your eyes you might see bears in the design. Madoc gave a loud knock on the door.

The soldiers had stopped an old man and woman, and were poking their swords into a cart of freshly washed laundry. Madoc banged again. 'Help me,' he said. Aoife twisted the handle.

'Halt!' The soldiers were a dozen houses away.

'It's locked!' Aoife said. She shoved hard at the door. The commander's voice, so loud, made her jump. 'You men search that way! You lot come with me! March on!'

Aoife peeped out of the portico, then jerked back. The soldiers were coming. She put her hands over her ears.

Tramp tramp tramp. That sound, of hard metal studs

ringing on the ground, was like hammer blows. Roman soldiers, after her. Tramp tramp tramp.

In the peace of Tessius's villa, she had pushed the memory out of her mind. Now it burst out, taking her back to the day, four years before, when the soldiers had come.

'Madoc! Mad-oc! Maa-ddoc!' The cries of their nurse, Anwyn, down in the settlement, was all the warning they had. Racing down from the top of the hill, Aoife made Madoc stop as they were about to enter the dun. It was on fire. Flames jumped from roof to roof. Roman soldiers drove people and horses before them.

Behind them, her brother Ewan flung his arms wide, as if to shield them. 'Run!' he cried. 'Run! Run—' His cry was stopped by the thud of a Roman spear in his back. Aoife had seized Madoc and jumped into the ditch that surrounded the settlement, running faster than she had ever run before. The Mother spoke to her: *'Go to the grove. Go to Bevis.'*

Darting over the hill, through the trees, they had eluded the soldiers. No one had followed them to their father's grove, deep in the wood. There was thin smoke rising from the hut. Dimock, the servant, must be late baking the bread.

They stepped into the sacred glade. Dimock's body lay across the entrance to the hut. Another body lay behind him, in the shadows, one bare foot poking out into sunlight, like part of a wax effigy dropped by accident.

'Stay back!' Her sister Igren had appeared from the hut, her clothes torn, her face smudged with blood. She stepped into the sunlight. She carried a sword.

'My father!' Aoife threw herself into the hut. Bevis's

body lay there with two others, Roman soldiers. She saw a helmet, crushed by a single blow from a sword. Her father's dead face was as grey as wood ash.

'Go to the river! Find Brec! Look after Madoc!' Igren shouted, flourishing her sword as she ran back to the dun. Aoife never saw her sister again.

While Madoc pushed at their father's body, as if to wake him, Aoife had picked up the staff lying next to the entrance and prised off the bronze badge at its top, the mark of the Mother, Edain. A resolve, hard as iron, rooted itself in her mind: to avenge the deaths of her father and brother.

'*Go to the river . . . Find Brec!*' She had grabbed Madoc and run, but as they left the grove, Roman soldiers had closed on them. Weaponless, Madoc had whirled round on them like a trapped hornet, lashing out with his fists. They were too strong.

Aoife and Madoc were not killed, but sold into slavery. On the journey to Rome they saw many tribesmen, with many brands, but none from the tribe of Edain. No one recognized them. No one knew who they were. They were children, slaves, anonymous, stateless, without rights, without names. Yet the Mother watched over them and kept them safe. Until now.

'Halt!' The harsh sound brought Aoife back to the present. Cra-assh. The soldiers stood to attention.

Again came the shout: 'Slaves of Tessius Maximus! Come out! Come out!'

Aoife thumped the door with both fists.

'You men—check every house! Yes, I know everyone's asleep! Wake 'em up! Get on with it!' Tramp tramp tramp.

Aoife thought her arms would break, when, with a jerk, the door finally gave way. Two sharp black eyes appeared in the gap. The door was flung open and they were bundled inside.

CARPUS ALEXANDER

The smell of rotting flesh added to the nausea simmering in her stomach. Retching, as if to vomit all her memories, Aoife pressed her hand to her mouth.

'Why have you come here?' The man addressed Madoc. 'Why did you not wait, as arranged? My servant would have collected you.'

'He did not come—'

Their host pushed them before him down a passage into the house, as the soldiers arrived and banged on the door.

Laying a finger to his lips, the man went to speak to them. Aoife pressed herself into the shadows.

'Search my premises, by all means!' he said. 'I have a fresh consignment just delivered—leopard and boar—so I would ask you to make as little sound as you can and no threatening gestures. I'm harbouring no runaways—' The man laughed, sounding quite innocent. 'Justinius, my friend! I can hardly believe the news—Tessius Maximus dead?'

There was a further brief conversation, but the soldiers did not enter the house, and when they left the man bundled Aoife and Madoc on, into a dismal room.

The taint of decay was strong here: heaps of animal pelts

lay on the floor, lining the walls, some with heads, some without: wolf and deer, fox, bear and others, of a kind Aoife had never seen. There were parts of animals too: horns and claws, hooves, and tails like dried twisted sticks.

'Why did you leave the villa?' Furious, the man splashed wine into a cup and drank it in one swallow. 'You were meant to go straight to the ship. You should not have come here!'

'Tessius is dead! Murdered! I didn't know what to do, or what might happen to us!' Madoc cried. 'No one came for us, then I saw a chance and took it!'

The stranger pointed to a bench next to a table in the middle of the floor. 'Sit!'

Madoc sat, but Aoife remained standing and looked out of the window into a courtyard surrounded by closed doors. There were animals here, in this enclave, she could sense them; live ones, miserable ones, making no sound.

'Well, Rufius!' The stranger offered Madoc a cup of wine. Aoife looked at him: *Rufius was the name given to Madoc by their master, Tessius.* 'You are now in my hands—' Over the rim of his cup, he glanced with predatory eyes at Aoife—'and your sister.' With an attempt at courtesy, he inclined his head in a greeting. 'For the time being, you are safe,' he said, 'but, from now on, you must obey orders.'

'*Orders?*' Aoife said.

A succession of howls drew the stranger's attention to a back room. 'Pour your sister some wine,' he said to Madoc, as he left.

'How do you know this man?' Aoife said.

'He's a friend of Mistress Lucilla,' Madoc said. 'You must have seen him visiting whenever Tessius was away?'

'You mean—' Aoife raised her eyebrows and Madoc nodded.

'What has he promised you?'

Madoc's face reddened at the tone of warning in Aoife's voice.

'He's a friend! He's sympathetic to the rebel cause and believes Rome should leave Britannia to rule itself! He's offered us a change of clothes, food, weapons—'

'—and safe passage home.'

'Yes!'

The cries from the back room fell silent at the lash of a whip and the man returned.

'New arrivals take time to settle,' the stranger said. He looked at Aoife.

'Flavia, isn't it? Sister to Rufius here.' *I never acknowledged that name*, Aoife thought. His eyes were appraising her body, as if she were on sale in the forum. *He has the empty smile of a slave trader.*

'Welcome, friends,' said the man. Unblinking, Aoife met his stare. *You are my enemy.*

There were olives and bread on the table, which their host invited them to share. 'Welcome to the house of Carpus Alexander! I am he—merchant, and, by Royal Appointment, supplier to the Imperial Court of Rome.'

Aoife's stomach canted as the man went on, 'I trade in animals, my dear. Dead or alive. There is a beast for every purpose: for meat, for breeding, for public entertainment. I have beasts who will rip out each other's throats!'

Sourness rose to the back of her throat and the man laughed at her expression. *He enjoys my discomfort.*

'I supply live beasts for the circus, for funeral games and such, here in Rome.'

He drank more wine and put down his cup. 'My speciality is exotics—those rare creatures that make the spectators dig out their coin and pay to gaze at, in wonder. Have you ever encountered the manticore? Or the hydra? Or the basilisk, eh?' he said. 'The basilisk can turn men to stone, and has done so, in my shows at the circus.' The merchant picked up a scaly hide, bloodstained and torn, and held it out for Aoife to examine. 'Sphinx. The very best Egyptian.' He laughed as she twisted away from such a pitiful object.

'I have seen dragons from the centre of the earth—Yes!' He nodded solemnly. 'They have all passed through my hands.' He put down the hide. 'People like something different. I satisfy their demands.'

The man gazed into mid-air, as if seeing himself receiving the adoration of the crowd. He picked his teeth. *He believes his own lies.*

Oooww-oooooohhhh, howled some poor creature. Carpus Alexander went to the door.

'Deal with it, Vidius!' he shouted, but his servant summoned him, and, with a curse, he again left the room. Aoife followed the trader to the door and watched him walk to the end of a long narrow corridor. The left side of the otherwise bare passage was lined with cages, stacked one on top of the next. Between the cages were larger pens, some empty, some occupied.

At the far end was a door, partly open. It gave on to the street outside. Aoife caught a glimpse of masts and sails. *Boats. The river.* She whispered to Madoc.

'We must leave. This man won't help us: he is a trader. We're goods to sell to the highest bidder.' She looked down the corridor to the open door. 'I'd rather take my chance on the streets.'

'He knows Anwyn!' Madoc said.

Aoife swung round. '*Anwyn?*' Was it possible? Was their nurse still alive?

Carpus Alexander returned. He took up his cup of wine and drank.

'My brother tells me you met a Celtish woman in Britannia, by the name of Anwyn,' said Aoife.

'I did indeed. Anwyn, of the household of Caradoc. She longs to see you again.'

'Is she well?'

'Last time we met, very well.'

'And her son?' Aoife ignored Madoc's stare of surprise. Anwyn was childless.

'There was a young man. What was his name? Er . . . '

'Kynann,' Aoife said, plucking a name from the air to bait the trap which would expose the trader's deception.

'Of course, Kynann. They were both well, when I was last in Britannia.'

Liar. 'When was that?' said Aoife.

Carpus banged down his cup.

'No more questions.'

There was a dangerous edge to his voice.

'Get up, Madoc, we're leaving,' Aoife said, moving to the door.

'Not yet,' said the trader. He seized her arm and pushed her down on to the bench next to Madoc, then picked up a small woven basket and placed it before them.

'You have taken me by surprise, Rufius. You should have waited at the villa.'

'But Tessius is dead!' said Madoc. 'The household is in uproar! Lucilla thinks he was poisoned!'

Carpus took the lid off the basket. 'Tessius was a fool.'

He reached into a leather pouch hanging on the front of his toga and brought out a small snake, yellow and black, its tongue tasting the air. With an assured grip, he held it aloft, between finger and thumb of his right hand.

'There, there, little one,' Carpus addressed the snake. 'You must rest now, after a task well done.' Aoife fixed her eyes on the snake as the trader held it a hand's breath from her face.

'*Vipera aspis*,' murmured Carpus, 'the common asp. Its bite is deadly.'

'You killed Tessius!' Aoife cried.

Time froze, as if the sand had stopped running through the hour glass. 'Madoc!' Aoife shouted and ran for the door. In a swift move, Carpus blocked their way. He held out the snake, threatening them with its bite. Aoife stood her ground. 'You show no fear—very good, very good!' said the trader.

'Get back!' Madoc cried, pulling out the knife with the gold filigree hilt.

'Don't be foolish, Rufius. If you harm me, my servants will hand you over to the soldiers. Is that what you want?' For answer, Madoc lowered the knife. 'A wise decision,' said the trader. 'Now, sit.' He nodded to the bench. Having no choice, Aoife and Madoc slowly seated themselves.

24

Carpus looked at the knife, shrugged, and placed the snake in the basket.

'My knife!' said Carpus. 'Wherever did you find it?'

'In Tessius's chamber, by his bed,' said Madoc.

'Ah. I must have dropped it. You guessed well, I admit it, I did kill Tessius, and he deserved his fate: he reneged on our bargain. He would have *given* you to the emperor— free of charge, gratis—in return for the *possibility* of becoming a senator. Was that *ever* going to happen?' Carpus laughed out loud. 'I offered him gold, for the two of you, spawn of Caradoc's blood: I paid dear for you. We had an agreement!' He pressed his hand to his chest. 'You were mine! Then, at dawn *today*, at the very last minute, knowing my ships were ready to depart, he sent word that he had *changed* his mind. Poor foolish Tessius.'

'You can't keep us here!' Aoife cried, attempting to stand. Carpus pushed her back into her place.

'Consider the facts, my dear. One: Tessius is dead. Two: you are runaway slaves. Three: I am a respectable citizen, and the emperor trusts me. If you attempt to escape, I shall have the soldiers on to you within fifty paces. And what will they believe? That I killed Tessius or that you did? Rufius, put down the knife.' Madoc laid the knife on the table.

'If they take you from this house, I shall make sure that you are condemned for the murder, then it will be the nails and the cross, or a mad dance in the Circus, dodging the lion's jaws . . . "*I'm innocent! I'm innocent!*" you will cry to your last breath and no one will listen to you, for who listens to a slave?'

'We'll go to the emperor! He will take us as hostages!' Aoife cried, her voice faltering. It was her last feeble hope and a cold slick of sweat filmed her skin, as Carpus dismissed it, laughing.

'Claudius will crush you like flies. He seeks to eliminate you, while making sure that Caradoc hears that you were found after all these years, alive, in Rome, but were, unfortunately, executed.' He gestured to the food on the table. 'Come! Why talk of such things?' he said. 'Eat! Drink! Forget Tessius. Forget the emperor.'

With a sudden gesture, he leaned towards Aoife and ran his finger down her cheek. 'You're quite safe with me. No one will find you here.'

Carpus snapped the lid on to the snake basket and secured it with strong leather ties.

THE WOLF

'I shall take you back to Britannia,' the trader went on, 'and claim ransom, myself, from Caradoc. Claudius is not a trader, he does not understand business.' He gestured to a pile of dirty rags in the corner of the room. 'You may sleep there tonight. I shall move you to Ostia, at dawn, to the ships. For the duration of the voyage, you will live on board with the other slaves.'

'*Slaves?*' Madoc shouted. 'You said—'

'Take it or leave it. This is a risky enterprise. The emperor is searching for you. My servants are already out in the city, spreading the word that you are on your way south, to divert his attention. You cannot stay in Rome: your only chance of survival is to come with me, under his nose, north to Britannia.'

Aoife jerked away as Carpus's fingers darted forward to touch the brand on her neck. 'That mark is being chalked on house walls all over the city. Best keep it covered.' Aoife rubbed away the touch of his fingers.

'I warn you, trader, you will pay dear for harming us—' she said.

'Brave words, Druid, though foolish.'

Carpus took a couple of olives from the bowl on the

table and nibbled at them like a rodent, before spitting the stones onto the floor.

A shout came from the corridor. He left the room.

Aoife bent towards Madoc. 'We're leaving. We'll find somewhere to hide until dark, then move down river.' She reached for the trader's knife, then drew back as he returned and, instead, picked up her cup of wine.

He picked up his own cup, sniffed it, then raised it in salutation: 'To profit!' he said. 'And successful bargaining!' He drank deeply from his cup and waited until Aoife had sipped from hers. 'I'm glad that you have decided to be sensible,' he said. He turned to Madoc.

'Rufius, it's a long journey to Britannia. As my personal slave, what services can you offer? Are you a scribe? Or a scholar? Do you read or write? Do you have the sight?' He leaned eagerly forward. 'Do you tell fortunes? You are the son of a Druid. Do you have your father's powers? Druids can predict winds and tides, they can look into the roots of time and say what is to come, who rises, who falls—' He thrust his hand under Madoc's nose, palm upwards. 'Tell my fortune, Rufius.'

Aoife gave Madoc an almost imperceptible nod, a signal he understood. He took the trader's hand and assumed a serious expression. While Madoc kept the trader busy, Aoife inched her fingers towards the knife. If Madoc could hold Carpus's attention for another moment, they would have a weapon and a chance to escape.

As her fingers curled over the hilt, something touched her foot. She jerked back as a shapeless grey lump, some hairy creature lying under the table, edged forward, to rest its nose on her toes. The lump raised its head: two bloodshot eyes looked up at her. *Wolf*. Aoife reached down to the hot dry nose. The wolf, tied by a chain around its neck, gave a soft growl and stretched towards her.

Carpus was still enthralled with Madoc's fortune-telling; he had not noticed her reaching down, so Aoife laid her hand on the wolf's sticky brow, between his ears, to listen to his mind, to search for the sickness that afflicted him. *There*. Its dark red centre was an infected blister behind his left ear. Chafed by the chain, it burned and gnawed at him without respite.

Steady . . . steady . . . The wolf responded to her thoughts with a cautious glance. *There, boy, good boy . . .* The wolf did not growl or bare his teeth as she reached for the chain.

'What are you doing?' Carpus shouted.

'He deserves better than to be kept chained up here in this filthy den!' Aoife retorted. 'He has been a hunter all his life, faithful and strong in his tribe—'

The wolf yelped as Carpus grabbed the chain from her hand.

'Stop that—' Madoc cried, '—Aoife can treat the wolf and perhaps make him well again! See for yourself, he doesn't threaten her—'

Carpus let go of the chain, shrugged, and stepped back. He kept his eyes on Aoife as she encouraged the wolf out into the light.

'I'll need salt water and oil—any oil, as long as it's fresh.' She passed her hand over the wolf's back, with calming gestures. The trader gestured to Madoc to pass Aoife the things she had asked for.

'He lies like a lamb at your feet,' he murmured, as the

wolf submitted to the treatment. The trader's eyes glittered and flashed. 'You *charm* him,' he breathed. '*You* have the gift—'

Ignoring the trader, for she neither saw nor heard anything round her while she treated the wolf, Aoife went on stroking the bristly place between its ears. The wolf was grateful for the healing, but she knew that his great spirit had already begun its last journey. At last she sat back and breathed again.

'Treat him with kindness. Feed him,' she said.

'By all the gods—' Carpus squealed with delight, '*you're* the Druid.' His voice rose with excitement. 'I have a *Druid*—'

'Food!'

Carpus seized a meaty bone from a chest, and threw it to the wolf.

'That's no good,' Aoife said, handing it back, 'he needs broth or gruel, something soft. His jaw aches.'

Carpus allowed Madoc to prepare suitable food, then, at Aoife's request, went to speak to Vidius about cleaning out a pen for the wolf, who was now freed from his chain. When the trader had left the room, Aoife darted to the door, pressed herself to the wall and peered down the passage. Carpus was making urgent gestures, towards where she was standing. Vidius nodded his head vigorously. Behind them, the outer door swung open. Two slaves carried in crates of fruit.

'Watch for my signal!' she hissed to Madoc, darting back to her place next to the wolf.

When the wolf was safely settled into his pen, Carpus approached Aoife. 'Are you able to treat all animals in this way? Bears, hounds, horses?' His eyes glittered, his mouth worked as he moistened his lips. Aoife's face must have told him what he longed to know, because he burst into loud laughter and rubbed his hands. 'Tessius had no idea of what he had under his roof! I would have paid a hundred times his asking price! You have the gift! I can hardly believe it!' The trader spread his arms wide and looked up to the ceiling. 'Thanks to great Jupiter!'

He looked at Aoife. 'Why go back to Britannia? Why not stay here?' He held her jaw and whispered, with foul breath, into her face. 'We'll have to take that mark off your neck. There'll be a scar, of little importance to a whey-face like you. Your hair—' He grimaced. 'I'll cut it. It's the best I can do. We'll darken it with Egyptian dye. I have some, it cost me dear, made from putrefied ox liver. I'm told it works very well.' He let her go. 'You would live in this house, in charge of the premises. I would provide for your every need. In fact, we could marry! How would you like to be the wife of a citizen?' He gripped her arms.

Aoife pulled away. 'Never!' she said. She pushed her arms up and wide, breaking the trader's grip. She ran to the passage, but Carpus stepped in front of her. 'Such courage, such fire! I must have you!'

With a strong kick to his shin, Aoife ran to the corridor. 'Madoc!' she cried.

'There before you!' Madoc shouted, darting into the passage ahead of her.

At the end of the passage, Vidius was walking out of the door, his arms full of baskets. As he disappeared, sunshine flooded in, like clean water. Madoc flew through the door. Aoife was passing the wolf pen when Carpus caught up with her. He swung her round, then let her go and fell, as, with its last burst of strength, the wolf broke from its cage. Aoife accepted its gift as it struggled with the trader: the few moments she needed to escape.

As she hurried along the quay, she felt the wolf's fleeing spirit brush against hers. It had lost its fight. Behind them, Carpus Alexander blundered out of his house, wielding his bloody knife.

'IF I CAN SAVE YOU, I WILL.'

'In here!' Madoc dragged her into the shade of a stack of cloth bales. Crouching next to him, Aoife laid her hot cheek against the coarse hessian. 'He won't find us here.' Behind was a maze of stacked crates, boxes, and barrels.

Aoife risked looking out at the vessels lining the river bank, bumping together with a clatter and clink of chains. Men were carrying cargo on board, and, on each boat, hoisting aloft the emperor's flag. The fleet was being prepared for the voyage across the Great Sea to Gaul, the first stage on the journey to Britannia. What if they gave themselves up? Would the emperor take them back to Britannia? If they reached the stronghold, surely Caradoc would rescue them—

She slumped against the bale. They could not move yet. They must wait, until the trader abandoned the search, perhaps for the next hour or two. Time to rest. She couldn't rest. There were too many unanswered questions. If Carpus was right about the emperor, who else might help them? Who would befriend two runaways? Who would shelter British rebels?

She rubbed the mark on her neck, then pulled her red-gold hair loose of its Roman plait, until it splayed around her shoulders like a shawl and covered her mark.

'Soldiers!' Madoc hissed, at the tramp-tramp of marching feet. Aoife's mind raced over their scant options. She glanced again at the jetty: guards were now searching every bale, every barrel.

'Slaves of Tessius Maximus! Come out of there!' The shout stabbed her like a dart.

As she tried to pull Madoc deeper into the maze of cargo, she dislodged a pile of baskets. 'Come out! Now!' A soldier pushed the cargo aside and, using his spear, forced them into the street.

One of the emperor's Praetorian Guard, his personal escort, stared down at her. Sunlight flashed on his golden helmet. 'Thank the Mother I have found you,' he murmured.

Aoife's eyes widened as she looked into eyes as blue as her own and heard words spoken in her own Celtish tongue. She pressed her lips tightly closed to prevent calling out in a rush of joy.

The soldier looked furtively around, then reached out to examine the mark on her neck, then on Madoc's. 'Forgive me, I had to be sure,' he said. He helped them to stand. 'Aoife, Madoc—son and daughter of the Druid Bevis, blood kin to Lord Caradoc—I am your servant,' he said with a formal bow. 'If I can save you, I will.'

'Who are you?' said Aoife.

'In Rome I'm Justinius,' he said. 'But my birth name was Huw, son of Erian. Our fathers were friends.'

'You're from Gaul! I remember Erian!' Aoife said.

'No more questions,' said Justinius, as more soldiers arrived. 'Trust me. I must take you to the emperor. Don't be afraid.'

He pushed Aoife and Madoc towards the main thoroughfare, his expression now one of iron efficiency. Staring coldly ahead, he herded his prisoners into the middle of the square of soldiers, so that they were well guarded on all sides, then gave the order to march to the emperor's headquarters.

'It's the law court!' Madoc whispered, as their guards stamped to a halt at the foot of a flight of steps. It led up into a portico, the grand entrance to the court where civil cases were heard. Aoife knew that the emperor himself sometimes sat in judgment. Someone pushed her and she stumbled up the steps. They halted in the shade of the portico.

When the door opened and passwords were exchanged, she followed Justinius inside the building, with Madoc close behind with his escort. They entered a cool tiled entrance hall.

There was a guard on every door and many doors in the large vestibule. Straight ahead was a long corridor, open on one side to what might be a pleasant courtyard: sunlight shone between columns. Shadows of leafy branches, moved by a breeze, played on the tiled floor. She could hear bird song. A man, seated at a table in one corner, called Justinius forward to state his business, then after a brief exchange of words, signalled with his stylus that they were to go on into another room.

The next room was smaller and warmer. There were statues of the gods ranged round the walls in niches: blank-eyed Jupiter, Minerva, and Mercury with his winged sandals.

They were told to wait. She was tired. Her eyes closed. She dreamed of a bed with a pillow, and no one to tell her to get up.

Echoing footsteps. Aoife opened her eyes. A senator, dressed in a white toga with a purple border, adjusted the folds of his robe. 'Come!' he said. They were led into yet another chamber.

This room was open on the left side to a garden, with access via steps down from a pillared colonnade. A fountain splashed there, over a marble statue of the god Pan, playing his pipes; a peaceful sound, yet Aoife shuddered: the atmosphere in this room was full of dread. It permeated the air, an invisible dense energy that took her courage away.

Soldiers stamped to attention as a man moved from the shadows to a marble desk set on a dais raised across one corner of the room. He was slight in figure, and rocked with a swaying gait as he made his way to his seat behind the desk. Aoife's heart thrilled with fear as the man clutched the gold-braided edge of his purple robe, as if to stop himself falling. This man was the Emperor Claudius. He held their lives in his hands.

'Hail, Caesar!' Justinius gave a sharp salute, which Claudius acknowledged with a desultory wave. 'We have captured—'

As Claudius raised his forefinger, Justinius jumped to attention and fell silent. The whole room seemed to hold its breath as the emperor looked at the first of a pile of scrolls on his desk. Aoife felt the threat in this gesture: something terrible was about to happen.

Claudius tilted his head and a slave, standing like a

statue against the wall, was brought forward between two guards. One of them seized his right hand and positioned it on the edge of the desk. The slave, shaking with terror, muttered the same words over and over. Aoife could not make them out.

In a soft voice, the emperor read aloud from the scroll: 'Theft of cloth which was then used for wiping mud from his feet.' He glanced at the slave with a sneer of distaste. 'You understand your crime?' he asked. 'You know its punishment?' The slave made no answer. Still muttering, he stared at the floor.

'Justinius,' said Claudius. It was a command.

Justinius walked to the slave, drew his sword and, with one clean sweep, cut off the man's right hand. Aoife groaned and covered her eyes. Behind her, Madoc gripped her shoulder, as guards took the victim away and slaves hurried forward to clean up the site of judgment.

Justinius cleaned his sword, then sheathed it and stood to attention by the emperor's desk. For the first time, Claudius glanced at Aoife and Madoc, then murmured to Justinius, who clipped a salute and left the room.

As the dread silence settled over the room again, Aoife jerked back her shoulders. It was as if the Mother had spoken directly to her: *Do not die here without a fight. There is nothing to lose.*

'Caesar!' she called. Her voice sounded shrill to her ears. She swallowed hard before going on. 'How long must we be kept waiting?'

As a guard stepped towards Aoife, Claudius gestured to the soldier to stand down. 'What did you say?'

'I asked how long we were to be kept waiting,' Aoife

said, focusing on saying the words without trembling. It took her every full-stretched nerve to face the emperor.

He left his desk. 'Do you address me, slave?' he said, in a dangerously quiet tone.

Aoife stuck out her chin. 'Caesar, I am no slave. My name is Aoife. I am daughter of the Druid Bevis, of the house of Caradoc, whom you call Caratacus. My mother was Caradoc's sister. I am his kin.'

'Are you wise to admit it?' Claudius said. The emperor's cruel eyes impaled her as if on a stake. 'Bow to your master,' he said.

She gathered her courage. 'I will not. I have endured four years of servitude and a childhood lost. I will bow to no man ever again.'

'Aoife!' She was aware of Madoc's cry, but did not respond to it. Instead she held the emperor's gaze.

'Two scions of the house of Caratacus.' Claudius chuckled. 'Your uncle dares to call himself the king of Britannia. I'm on my way to point out his error.'

A trumpet sounded and a party of senators swept into the room, all wearing white togas with purple braid.

'What brings the senate to disturb my conversation?' the emperor asked. A grey-haired senator stepped forward.

'Caesar, your ships lie ready, in Ostia. And there's good news from Gaul. Aulus Plautius has moved to the coast with the Ninth Legion. The Second and the Fourteenth join them there. By now they will have begun the invasion.'

'And the Twentieth?'

'Up to full strength, battle ready.' The senator unfurled a scroll and began reading: 'The Twentieth Legion, the Valeria, joins the invasion force in northern Gaul, at

Gesoriacum, and begs leave to set up camp there on the plain—'

'Granted—granted—' Claudius said with a dismissive gesture. 'Is that all?'

'There is a personal message from Aulus Plautius. He will await your arrival on the far side of the Thames. After the defeat of the rebels, he will accompany you into the stronghold.'

'Lord Caradoc will not be defeated so easily!' Aoife cried. The emperor looked round, with a quizzical look, as if his hound had burst into speech.

'Caradoc will drive Rome into the sea!' added Aoife. Shouting helped her to control her fear.

Claudius laughed out loud. 'You have spirit. I shall look forward to your execution.'

Justinius came back into the room, accompanied by a British chieftain, dressed in plaid breeches and tunic, as if he came to address his own tribe. Aoife's eyes widened. 'Verica!' she said. *Traitor. Verica, Caradoc's enemy, who had accepted the rule of Rome and opened the gates of Britannia to the invaders.*

Claudius nodded his satisfaction. 'It seems the slave knows you. Can you identify them? Speak, Verica! If these two are Caratacus's kin, they may be of use to us. Do you know them?'

'It's a long time since I saw them.'

'Why would they make such a claim, risking death, if it were not true?'

Verica shrugged, then with a sudden gesture, reached forward to push Aoife's hair aside, exposing her mark. She jerked away from his rough fingers.

'She bears the mark of Edain,' exclaimed Verica. He gripped Aoife's jaw and wiped three fingers along the lines below the horse head tattoo. 'She was spawned by Bevis on Caratacus's sister, who died giving birth to her.' As he pushed her away, Aoife's paralysing fear turned to while-hot anger. She spat at him and wished her spittle were deadly poison. Calmly, Verica wiped it from his face. 'She has Bevis's fire! I believed the whole family killed when I laid waste to their father's hold and brought his gold to swell the Imperial coffers.'

'*You!*' Aoife sprang at Verica. A soldier caught her and knocked her to the ground.

The emperor laughed. 'So the trapped wasp, facing death, still uses its sting.' He moved to the door. 'Dine with me, Verica.'

Verica's eyes bored into Aoife's. She did not look away. 'Kill them now,' he said.

'No, I want to see the look on the face of Caratacus when he sees me march into his stronghold with his sister's brood as my prisoners.'

'I would kill them. Kill the boy first. I could do it now for you.' Verica drew his sword.

'NOOooo!' Aoife shouted. She raised her fists, and, using them together, struck Verica a blow on the side of the head. Caught off-balance, he stumbled and knocked his head against the corner of a marble plinth supporting a bust of the goddess Minerva. Felled like a tree, he clawed at the emperor. Blood, from a deep cut on the left side of his brow, smeared the emperor's toga, as Verica sank to the floor.

A guard put his knife to Aoife's throat. Justinius dragged Verica, pale and still, away from the emperor's feet.

'The wasp stings again,' Claudius called. 'Justinius, take our friend to the infirmary and make sure he has all due attention.' He took off his soiled toga and handed it to a slave. A second slave, head bowed, held out a red cloak to Claudius. The emperor, wearing only his white tunic, threw the cloak hastily round his shoulders. He spoke to Aoife.

'The boy goes to Britannia, where I shall take great pleasure in his execution, which will be a grand affair, in the presence of Caratacus. Say goodbye to your brother: you have sealed your own fate.' He looked at a guard. 'Give her to Damianus.'

Aoife caught Madoc's eyes, bright with disbelief, as he was led away. She managed a shaky smile.

'The Mother keep you safe!' she shouted, as she too was led away, by a different door. 'Look for me! I'll find you!' What made her shout such a promise? It was her last thought before the soldier's fist closed her mouth.

DAMIANUS

Damianus. Aoife had heard the name. She tried to remember as she was hurried out of the courthouse and into the street. When the imposing facade of the Circus Maximus rose before her and she was pushed in through the felons' entrance, with a paralysing flash of terror she remembered. Damianus was the keeper of the wild animals that criminals faced in the arena. Lions, tigers, bears, wolves, and others she could not name had all passed by the villa, in their cages, on their way into Rome.

Everyone in the kitchen had fallen quiet when the fanfare of trumpets sounded out across the city, signalling the start of the games. On Quintus's orders the shutters were always left open and must never be closed. No amount of loud talk could mask the raucous cheers of the crowd, and the roars of the animals, or the howls when they were beaten back or wounded.

Damianus. When she was ushered into his presence, the animal keeper barely looked up from his supper. Then, when Aoife's Praetorian escort had left, having officially handed her over as a criminal for due punishment, he muttered, 'Lions have already eaten. Shame. At least with them there's no mess to clean up afterwards. Cerberus would have dealt with this one and not a scrap left.'

Was it her silence that finally made him look at her? Aoife saw the keeper's eyes flick to the mark on her neck, then back to her face.

'Celt, are you?' he said. 'The slave boy, Brennius, is Celt. He'll look after you. Don't bother trying to talk to him though, he's deaf.'

With a wave of his roast boar rib, Damianus signalled to the slave to approach. A thin pale boy, with black hair and large blue eyes, rose up like a ghost and came to stand in front of Aoife.

Damianus pointed with his knife down the passage. 'Take her to the big stable. There's a new beast, just arrived, young and angry, from north Africa. A kill might be just what it needs to calm itself. Leave the girl in there with it. If she survives, which I doubt, we'll add her to the list for the next event, which will be—' He glanced at a wax tablet on which a slave was making marks, 'Funeral games,' he read, 'in honour of—who is it? Oh yes . . . Tessius Maximus. Is he dead then? Well, I never. Mm.'

The slave gestured to Aoife to follow him. When she stood her ground, someone gave her a hard shove in the back.

'Don't struggle, Celt,' Damianus shouted after her, as she stumbled after Brennius through the door. 'You'll only make matters worse.'

The pale slave, Brennius, suddenly smiled at her with his eyes—a light in the dark—as he kicked the door shut behind them, then led her on down a twisting flight of steps and along a stinking tunnel.

They passed gloomy rooms where gladiators lived, lit by narrow rays of sunlight through barred grilles above

44

their heads. She exchanged a brief glance with one man and saw his tired eyes, white slits in his dirty face.

They arrived at the stables. The doors to these were all shut tight, but there was a gap at the top of all the walls in this area to allow the circulation of air throughout the complex and she could hear heavy breathing and low threatening growls, the sounds of large animals eating, crunching bones.

Fighting her own terror, Aoife felt their fear and pain and confusion. These animals knew they were prisoners: they were desperate to find their way home. They were very angry.

She started as a lion roared, but the slave did not falter, leading her on to the very end of the passage, to the very last door, where he pulled out a knife and cut her bonds. He pushed open the door and prompted her to enter. When she hesitated, with surprising strength he pushed her inside, then shut and locked the door behind her.

IN THE ANIMAL PENS

She was in some kind of vaulted stable, dark and empty. She searched the shadows. She couldn't see any lions or tigers. *There's a new beast, just arrived, young and angry . . .* Damianus's words. With every part of her stretched tight as a drying hide, she strained to listen, but there was no hint, no stertorous breathing or shift of straw, or the sound of a wide lazy yawn, as a killer opened its jaws.

She walked to the other side of the empty stable, stepping in a sludge of old, damp straw, from which a smell arose: it was not unpleasing.

With a shaky smile, she clutched her hands to her chest. The smell reminded her of her father's stables at home where he had kept his own favourite horses, the pride of his heart. There had been twelve, each housing its separate occupant: Bedwyr, Arth, Mirain, Ialach . . . *Where were they now?*

She laid her hands flat on the wall, the chill stone easing the ache in her chest. How strange it was that a smell could bring back memories she thought she had pushed away for ever.

Above her head something moved: she snatched her hands away and looked up.

There was a row of small windows, open to the air. A

swallow flew in and out, threading the air like the shuttle on Anwyn's loom.

Below the windows, in the middle of the wall, was a gate of iron bars, which could be slid open, to the right, along iron grooves. Behind it, an arm's length away and hung on the outside, was a pair of wooden doors that led into the arena.

Presumably, during the Games, the outer wooden doors could be opened to display the beasts in the stable, who, though visible, were still safely caged. Perhaps the emperor then chose which beast his victims would face.

Aoife shivered. The sky was deep blue, on a golden afternoon. The cicadas were singing. At full stretch, she reached between the iron bars and banged at the wooden doors, but they were latched shut from outside with a plank and held firm. Light gleamed through a hole in the door on the right. Aoife pressed her face to the bars, to see through the gap.

She could see the empty Circus outside, the dusty track, still marked with the tracks of chariots. Small clumps of fine dried grass moved in the breeze; agh!—she stepped back in horror, realizing that it was not grass at all but animal fur. There was blood too, with fur or hair sticking to it.

Someone opened the inner stable door, dropped something inside, then slammed the door shut again. Aoife knelt to examine it: a bundle of dun-coloured cloth. Wrapped in the cloth was a skin of water, a loaf, and a knife, a Celtish blade. Who had left her these? The slave Brennius, her countryman?

She shook out the cloth. It was a length of fine woollen

weave, a welcome blanket to keep her warm. As she
threw it round her shoulders, there came a quiet tap on
the door.

'Who's there?' Aoife put her ear to the wood to listen.

'They are coming to put the beast in the stable.'

'Brennius?' *Or was it Justinius?* She shuddered, remembering the punishment meted out to the slave, and the way
in which the Praetorian had instantly obeyed orders and
cut off the man's hand. It was an act of terrible violence.
Could she trust someone who could do such a thing?

She was certain that the light in his eyes when he
found her with Madoc, beside the river, was a true light.
He had not been able to disguise it. If he did serve two
masters—Rome and Britannia—as she believed, perhaps
it was necessary to obey without question, even when the
order was so cruel. Perhaps this was a sacrifice he had to
make, to stay above suspicion. Someone tapped lightly at
the door.

'Mother save you—' she said, in thanks for the gifts.

'Prepare to defend yourself,' was the reply, then the
voice fell silent. She heard the sound of footsteps, going
back up the tunnel.

The plank on the arena doors was thrown up with a
crash. Aoife jammed the knife in her belt, then went back
to the iron gate. She waited on the left side of it, with her
back to the wall. When the cage was opened, perhaps she
could run into the arena. She held the knife with both
hands, out in front of her. She would not die without a
fight. She would not. Her knuckles turned white from the
effort of keeping the knife still. There would be one
chance—*Mother, if it is your will, let me live*. She glanced at

49

the doors. Something crashed into them. Once. Twice. Was it battering its way in? The doors rattled and shook, as if the earth itself trembled with terror, but no one opened them. What was taking them so long?

There came a low rumbling sound, the like of which she had never heard before in her life; thunder, but not thunder from the clouds, because it was made by a living creature. What creature made that sound, like the breathing of the earth itself? *Mother save me* . . .

The stable shook as the animal stamped and threw itself against the doors. Daylight disappeared from the crack, blocked by something outside. Wild shadows crossed the windows. How big was this beast?

Aoife lowered her knife as fear pinned her to the ground. Men shouted. There was the pounding of feet, men running. The doors shook and the creature roared, trumpeting as if the god Camulos himself was sounding his war horn. Again and again the doors shook. Then there was a different sound, the lash of whips, as the doors were finally thrown wide open.

A centurion barked orders, and soldiers, carrying spears, pushed the iron gate aside in its groove, then ran in and lined up on either side of the entrance. One shoved Aoife ahead of him, into the pen. She fell on to her knees. Then she turned to look up at the beast.

It was a giant, twice her height, three times her width, with legs broad as tree stumps and a huge head that thrashed in its cage of ropes, up and down, up and down, up and down. Half-naked slaves dragged it into the stable. One of its hind legs was bleeding.

There was a noisy splash and sharp smell as a stream

of urine issued from its rear. The slaves held their ground: soldiers, in the line of fire, yelped and jumped aside.

The centurion cracked his whip. The creature roared its trumpeting sound. Aoife's bones turned to water.

She stared at the creature and could not look away. A long nose projected from the front, like an extra limb, pliable and boneless. Besides its size and obvious strength, it had more weapons: two tusks, either side of its nose, like the tusks of a wild boar, curving to deadly points as long as a man's arm. The slaves holding the ropes watched the tusks warily as the beast tossed its head and angrily flapped its huge ears stretched wide on either side of its skull.

As the soldiers used spears to manoeuvre it, the creature threw back its head and roared its protest. The whip was used again, across its nose this time. It did the trick. The animal backed away from the stinging whip and stood still, making only a low rumbling noise as the soldiers secured the chains on its legs to iron rings in the wall.

'Soldiery—OUT!' was the command. The soldiers guarding the exit peeled away, one by one, into the arena.

'Everyone! OUT! You first.' The centurion pointed to the slave holding a rope attached to the beast's head. The man let the rope run to its length through his fingers, dropped it, then turned and ran for the doors. One by one the others followed him.

Aoife watched the panting beast as the stable was methodically emptied of the soldiers and slaves. The iron cage clanged as it was slid back into place. Light faded as the outer doors were shut and the plank dropped across them. She was left in the pen. She ran to the inner door, which led to the gladiators' pens, and tugged at the handle. It wouldn't budge. She was locked in.

As the creature turned its head to look at her, she slid down into the damp straw and let her knife fall from her limp fingers. The beast lifted one foot and stamped it hard on the straw. Its tiny black eyes glinted like flint in the gloom of the stable. Iron chains would not hold such a creature. Its foot would crush her like an insect. Aoife pulled the dun cloth slowly over her head and prepared to die.

The beast tugged at its chains. With a clang, one of the iron rings came away from the wall. Aoife sensed the sheer rage inside its head. It was watching her. Caged and in pain, it would surely take its revenge in the only way it could, on the only human being within reach. Clang. A second ring left the wall. Soon it would be free.

But time passed and nothing happened. The beast did not move. It uttered a low rumble. She opened her eyes.

The creature was still watching her. Its long nose unrolled and probed the air between them. It rumbled again, a deep, slow, soft sound in its throat. It kept its eyes on hers.

'Steady . . . ' Aoife said. Slowly she got up and extended her right hand to the beast. She held its gaze. Another iron ring fell from the wall and the beast shuffled its back legs. It moved towards her, then, before she could step aside, lowered its head and thrust at her with its terrible tusks. Once, twice.

'Great Mother protect me . . . ' she murmured. 'May I die well.'

She flinched, she couldn't help it, as the great tusks

swept towards her. Then she flinched again when the tip of the beast's nose gently touched her cheek, and spread the tears that were rolling down her face, in spite of her determination to stop them.

She opened her eyes. She was face to face with the beast. With a shock, she saw that it was also weeping. Liquid seeped from its eyes and crept down the side of its head. Gently it nudged her. Aoife touched its tears.

There was a sudden commotion outside. Aoife went to press her face between the iron bars, to peer through the gap into the arena. A detachment of soldiers was driving more of these beasts across the sand. She counted seven, then drew back as two men stopped directly outside. She recognized the emperor. He was pointing to the beasts.

'How can I ride any of these! They carry shame in their eyes! There must be magnificence when I ride into Caratacus's stronghold!' Slaves scattered as he made angry gestures. 'Where's the soothsayer? Has he even started the ritual yet? The new beast has been here for hours. I must know if this is the one I am to ride! I must have an answer.'

Thumping his fist into the palm of his hand, Claudius paced outside the stable, talking to himself, going over his plans as if to confirm them. 'I shall enter the stronghold alone, on my elephant. What better display of my power could there be? Towering above the rebels, I shall appear as a god! Six more will follow, in pairs, two by two. They shall all wear golden armour to follow their god in triumph! It will be—resplendent!'

He pinched his lower lip between finger and thumb.

'My beast will be the most magnificent, a creature repre-senting wild nature itself harnessed to my will.'

He realized that Damianus was watching him. 'The whole picture was revealed in the entrails! Great gods, where's that soothsayer? Is it too much to ask?'

'The new beast is magnificent, Caesar,' said Damianus. 'Her eyes blaze with regal pride!'

'Then I must have it! Where is it?'

'In this stable, dealing with that Celtish slave you sent.' Damianus put his ear to the door. 'The elephant is quiet now. They often are after the kill.'

Claudius rattled the latch on the doors.

'Caesar, please, don't provoke her! She could still prove dangerous!'

Aoife shrank back as Claudius peered through the gap. The beast roared and stamped its foot. The emperor started back.

'It can be tamed?'

'Certainly.'

Aoife looked at the beast—the el-e-phant. ' . . . *into the stronghold . . .* ' The elephant had a chance of going to Britannia. If only Madoc's plan had worked! His foolish, hopeful words pierced her memory—*'we're going home!'*— but he had been betrayed by the man he had trusted to help them. Their enemies had proved too strong and now she had no idea where Madoc was, or even if he was still alive. Dispirited by her thoughts, she folded them away in a box at the back of her mind. She closed the lid of the box and locked it tight. *If only*—what weak useless words.

'Clever you,' she said out loud, lifting her head to stare straight at the beast. She sniffed, then gave a shaky laugh.

'Clever you, to scare the emperor away. It's Britannia for you, you old el-e-phant.' The elephant lowered its head. Aoife pressed her cheek to the beast's.

'I wish I were going with you. Britannia's my home,' she murmured. 'I'm Aoife, of the house of Caradoc. Do you have a home? Do you have a name?'

She did not expect an answer, but a word came to her mind. *Bala . . . Bala . . .* and the picture of a young boy calling at the end of a very hot day. Dark-skinned, shading his eyes. *Africa.* A farmyard scudding with clouds of red dust. A barn roofed with palm. *Bala . . . Bala . . .*

The sound was so insistent and repeated, that she knew if the elephant did have a name, this was it.

'Bala. Bala,' she said, and was rewarded with a light touch of the elephant's nose and a low rumbling sigh of contentment.

Aoife stroked Bala's leathery hide, so deeply wrinkled, yet bristly and warm. 'You scared the emperor. Clever old you. Clever old you.'

In the arena, there was a busy clatter of sound: men shouting, animals braying, the grind of cartwheels, and the rattle of harness. Preparations were under way for the emperor's leaving. Had the soothsayer made a prediction about Bala? If they came for the elephant and found Aoife still alive, what would they do? Kill her at once? Or save her for the lions?

Terror made her hungry. She found the bread and water, and the knife, which she shoved into her belt.

On the point of sinking her teeth into the bread, she thought about Bala. The elephant stood patiently, one back leg still tied to the fourth and last ring in the wall, her huge head swaying to and fro, to and fro, as she dug into the straw with the tip of one tusk. Surely she was hungry, too, but one small loaf would not satisfy such a large animal. Aoife wasn't sure what an elephant ate. Hay perhaps, like her father's horses. She began a meticulous search of the pen.

In one dark corner she uncovered a water barrel. When she took off the lid, she saw green scum on the surface of the water and scraped it off, leaving clear water beneath. Stale or not, perhaps it would suffice, but she had nothing to carry it in.

If she could not take water to the beast, she must take the beast to the water. To do that, first she must free it from the ring.

It took a good while to work on the weakest part of the chain, but, by whittling away with her blade, she finally broke through it. Cupping her hand, she drew up some water from the barrel. Steadily, she carried it back to Bala.

'Come!' she called, holding out her hand and crooking the fingers of her other hand. The elephant watched her and made her soft rumbling sound, but she didn't move. 'Come!' Aoife repeated. Bala lifted her probing nose, and seemed to be smelling the air for a while. Finally she touched Aoife's hand. Aoife watched, amazed, as, using her long nose, she delicately sucked up the water. She showed Bala the barrel.

'It's here. Look.' Bala followed her and sank the tip of her nose into the scummy water. Aoife took up her own water skin and drank too.

When she began to eat her bread, Bala stopped drinking and, nuzzling behind the barrel and under a heap of what looked like old baskets, dragged out a sack of grain, then, behind that, a bale of hay. Aoife laughed and slapped her side. 'Clever you!' she shouted.

As the elephant ate, Aoife studied her strangeness: her long probing nose, her ears like sails, her tiny eyes fringed with the long lashes of a Roman beauty. Her brow was domed, parted into two bristly hillocks. Between them the skin was deeply scarred in a rough patch with uneven red edges. *Burned . . . you were burned . . .* Bala looked at her. Aoife saw the rage in her mind, the humiliation of submitting to the burning, to being captured.

The rear door into the stable was flung open. A troop of men entered. Dressed only in loin cloths and sandals, they were not soldiers. Not slaves either: they carried spears. Aoife looked at their scarred bodies: each man carried the marks of past battles, from wounds made by swords or spears or animal teeth and claws.

Gladiators. She stood quite still. Gladiators were worse than soldiers: they were murderers, bandits, criminals, granted a reprieve from the death sentence solely to provide entertainment in the arena.

The men lined up with their backs to the door. Behind them Damianus walked into the stable. Aoife faced him. Bala stood behind her, also facing him.

He seemed surprised to see Aoife alive. 'The gods smile on you, Celt,' he said, then he pointed to the elephant and issued his orders.

'Secure the beast!' he said. 'Hobble its legs with those chains. Make them tight this time.' As the men moved towards Bala, she gave a threatening grumble. Men picked up the chains.

As one of them jabbed Bala's leg with his spear, Aoife drew her knife and flung herself at him. Damianus snatched the knife, threw it across the pen, then caught her a blow that sent her reeling.

Falling, she caught the strange look on Damianus's face—regret? An apology?—then Bala roared. She threw out her long nose, curled it around Aoife under her arms, and lifted her on to her back.

Aoife thought her heart had stopped and started again. It was like riding a horse with a broad back, but from a much higher perch. She could reach up and touch the rafters. The men were all looking up at her, but she was safe. All she had to do was hold on. She settled herself behind Bala's ears, and clung on as the elephant lunged her tusks at the men.

The gladiators lowered their spears. Damianus was watching her. *Why doesn't he give the order to kill us?* she thought. *There are enough men for the job.*

The gladiators whispered to each other. Aoife heard the word 'witch', then again, 'Celtish witch'. Keeping their eyes on the elephant, they moved back to the door. Aoife realized the truth: they were afraid.

Their leader came to speak privately to Damianus. Some made signs with their hands, pointing at her with extended fingers, as if to ward off an evil spirit. Damianus drew his sword.

'By Jupiter, I shall have you all flogged! Call yourself fighters!' he sneered, then spat at their feet. 'Get her down!'

As the first man approached, Bala backed away into a corner of the stable where she was protected on three sides. 'Clever you,' Aoife whispered. There was no room for the men to attack. One or two might injure her, in a frontal assault, but only the leader came forward, and stood a spear's length away. Each time he attempted to come closer, Bala growled and lowered her tusks.

Damianus banged his fist to the wall. 'Get out, all of you! Get out now!' He drove the gladiators to the door and kicked them out. 'Scared of a Celtish witch? I'll deal with her myself!'

AN OFFER OF HELP

Damianus closed the door. He still held his sword high.

'Put down your weapon,' Aoife said. 'I'll come down. You must not hurt her.'

'Hurt her?' Approaching Bala, Damianus sheathed his weapon. 'I wouldn't hurt this one. Her road has been hard enough and may be again. The emperor's soothsayer has chosen her as the elephant he must ride into the rebel stronghold. She is going to Britannia.'

Damianus tapped the elephant's long nose. She lowered her head. 'Come, bring yourself on to her brow,' he said to Aoife. 'Hold on to her ear—that's right—now, let your body go limp. Push yourself down her trunk, her nose—that's it.' Aoife was surprised to find herself safely back on the firm earth. Her legs trembled.

'You know her?' she said.

'I know where she has come from and the family that mourn losing her—'

'She mourns too.'

In Damianus's clear blue eyes there was that look again. *Regret? Apology?* He bowed his head. 'My lady,' he breathed.

Aoife flushed. 'Why do you address me in this way?'

'Daughter of Bevis, you must listen to me. There's not much time.'

He jerked his head at the door. 'I am expected to kill you, but you must live, you must go back to Britannia, to join Lord Caradoc in the fight.'

'Who *are* you?'

'Four years ago, word came that you and your brother had survived an attack on your home settlement. I watched every slave sale in the market place, looking for the ones who bore the mark of Edain. You bear that mark. You also bear the sign of the Druid Bevis. Unmistakably, you are his daughter and blood kin to Caradoc. And your brother will be the next leader of the tribe of Edain. He is Bevis's heir.'

'My brother's a prisoner! He may be dead already!' Aoife spat the words.

'Madoc is alive.'

Aoife caught her breath. She hugged herself, trying to trust what Damianus was saying.

'He was put on board a transport, with reinforcements bound for Britannia. It has already left Rome. Don't trouble yourself: he has friends who watch over him.' Damianus put out his hand to comfort her, but Aoife moved out of reach.

'Why did you wait four years to help us?' she said, evenly.

'Four years ago I was a slave myself, though I was permitted to visit the market place, where I listened to the gossip and gathered the news. You were safe enough with Tessius, until he realized how useful you would be. I have watched you, and waited for the Mother to show us how to save you.'

'Us?'

Damianus glanced at the closed door, then banged his fist to his chest and muttered: 'I am not the only one to fight Rome from within its walls. Always, in head and heart, the fight goes on.'

Aoife pressed her lips together.

'You were born in Britannia?' she said. Damianus nodded.

'And your birth name?'

'Derryth.' Damianus gave a shaky laugh. 'Forgive me, I have not spoken that name out loud for many years.'

'Well, Derryth—'

'Damianus. The other is too dangerous to speak aloud.' He flinched at a sudden sound from the passage outside, then stood upright, stiff with tension, and, for the first time, Aoife saw that he was risking his life to speak to her.

'If I am not dead when your men return, what will they do?'

'I shall tell them that you have a gift with the elephant, that it obeys you. You will be offered to the emperor, to be its keeper, on the journey through Gaul to Britannia.'

'Do you have such power, to persuade the emperor to accept such an offer?'

'His soothsayer has declared this to be the beast which Claudius must ride. He needs a keeper for the beast on the journey across Gaul. Left alone with the elephant, you are unscathed. Look at her. She has made no move to attack either of us, yet she was brought here fighting every step of the way. I have a string of wounded slaves out there. In a short hour you have calmed her.

'I shall tell the emperor that you alone are capable of taking care of his elephant, but I must warn you: even if

63

he agrees, you will be in danger; his guards will be ready to kill you at any time, on his command. Will you take the chance?'

'I will.'

For a moment they fell silent, each deep in their separate thoughts. Then Aoife glanced again at Damianus's calm expression, and when, with a slight inclination of his head, he returned her smile, hope made her shiver. It was as if her spirit, like her body, were breaking free of its chains, like a butterfly freeing itself from its chrysalis prison. She prayed for the courage to keep her word.

'The emperor's procession is planned to take place after his victory,' she said. 'Is Caradoc defeated already?'

'He may have to accept defeat, for the time being. The emperor gathers an army of four legions, with auxiliaries—that's over forty thousand men in total. I doubt that Caradoc can field a quarter of that number.'

Outside, someone shouted:

'Damianus! More prisoners! What shall we do with them?'

Damianus shouted a reply. 'I'll be there soon. Tell Atticus to make a note.'

'If Caradoc is defeated, what can Madoc and I do?'

Damianus took her hand. 'You must return to Britannia, to lead your tribe. It will be a triumph for both of you, to return as prisoners of the emperor, then to take stand against him. Caradoc needs you and your brother. He may not win this time, but he will never give up fighting for Britannia's freedom. Your safe return will strike a heavy blow for the cause.'

'If I live to see my home again, what then? How shall I join my tribe? I will still be a prisoner.'

'Aoife, if you live to set foot on British soil, you will be rescued.' He waited for her response. *What choice do I have?* Aoife thought. *Any chance, however slim, is better than certain death.* She looked at Damianus and nodded. 'Very well.'

Damianus glanced at the door, then bent towards her. 'There is still the elephant to reckon with. She is not like the others: they will submit to the chains and the sting of the firebrand. Their eyes are dull, they are slaves, used to obeying. This one is different. She fights too: she dreams of going home.'

'You see that?' Aoife said. Damianus moved towards Bala, who lowered her head, at ease, and went on with her feed. He patted her cheek. 'I wish I could save every animal who comes to the Circus, but my job is to watch over them as they go to their deaths.'

Aoife stretched out her hand to him. He shrank back. 'I've made my bargain with Rome. I shall be a citizen in— let me see—another five years if I keep the slate clean.'

'Why do you want to be a citizen of Rome?'

'Because then I can marry, own my own land, control my destiny. There's nothing for me in Britannia.'

'The Mother's gift will never leave you.'

'I know it. When I've earned my citizenship, I shall leave the Circus and buy a farm. Then I shall use the skill bestowed by the Mother, to breed horses. Meanwhile—'

The door to the stable flew open. As the Emperor Claudius entered, Damianus stood to attention, all Roman again.

'Caesar, regarding this slave, I have a proposition to make,' he said.

FROM ROME TO GAUL

Just before dawn the next day, Damianus brought the news of the emperor's approval. 'No one else wanted the job! Claudius was relieved to find a keeper for his elephant, even a Celtish witch, especially when I told him how the beast had lifted you, unprompted, on to its back! You are to go with him to Britannia as keeper of the emperor's elephant!'

As Damianus laughed and repeated Claudius's words: '*If the Celt is still alive in the morning, she will accompany us to Gaul*', Aoife tried to share his pleasure, but when he finally left the stable, she felt heavy and dizzy. Nothing seemed real, yet it was real. The emperor's retinue was on the move, preparing to leave Rome. She would leave Rome.

Throughout the night, there had been the movement outside of animals and creaking store wagons being taken across the arena, on their way out of the Circus and down to the Tiber. They would come soon for Bala.

She straightened her clothing, then drank water and splashed her face. Bala had already dipped her trunk into the water butt, draining what was left, then set to eating the last bundle of hay.

Aoife turned away from the spy-hole into the arena and looked round the filthy pen for the last time. She was alive, she was setting off for Britannia. It was the first step.

Her thoughts flew to Madoc. Where was he? Crossing the sea or on dry land, marching northwards through Gaul?

Bala touched Aoife's arm with her trunk and Aoife went to her, and put her hand on the elephant's cheek. She moved closer, spreading her arms wide to embrace the side of Bala's head, one hand on her trunk, the other looped under her ear. Then she laid her head against the cushion of Bala's face, just under the cheekbone, as a picture grew clear in her mind. *Home*.

It was a place different from her own green hills, an arid place, with red dust and sparse vegetation. A single tree, huge, spread its shade over a wide area. Beneath its branches, elephants gathered to rest from the death-dealing heat of the day. Bala moaned again, a low mournful sound. *Home*.

Aoife stood back. Bala watched her. 'You want to go home,' Aoife said. 'As much as I do. You shall go. One day you shall.' As the daughter of a Druid, representative of the Mother, she would make a vow, a proper one.

She cleared her throat, gathered her breath, then laid her hand on Bala's trunk.

'By the Mother's sacred name, in the name of Edain— if it be Her will—I, Aoife, daughter of Bevis, swear that one day, you shall go home.'

Slowly she stroked Bala's bristly hide. She had made her vow: she must do all she could to keep it, though it seemed impossible. Bala had come from Africa, from the south. How was she to get Bala back there?

'I swear it,' she whispered, again, to comfort herself and, in the end, gave up striving for answers, trusting, as always, to the will of Edain.

When she had made another prayer for the hand of the Mother to shelter them, during the crossing of the Great Sea to southern Gaul, she repeated her vow to save Bala. 'A life for a life,' she said.

Men came into the stable, armed with ropes and spears, but Aoife told them to put them away. 'The elephant and I will go together,' she said. 'She will do as I ask.'

Aoife stood in front of Bala, who lifted her on to her back. She looked down at the men. 'Open the doors,' she said.

Transfixed, the men stared at Aoife. They shuffled their feet and made signs against evil spirits. *They do think I'm a witch*, she thought and her dry lips twitched into a smile. Eventually one of them, muttering words of protection, growled and went to obey the instruction.

Justinius strode into the stable. In his Praetorian voice, he spoke to Aoife: 'I shall be watching you, Celt, every step of the journey.' His words were coldly spoken, but there was a warmth in his eyes. 'There will be no nonsense about witchcraft.'

He addressed the men: 'By the emperor's orders, this slave is under my special protection. It's me you will have to face if she is harmed.'

Aoife watched him pick something up from the straw. It was the knife that Damianus had snatched from her. Justinius put it in his own belt, then his eyes drifted to the dun cloth tied around Aoife's shoulders, and she knew who had provided it for her. Justinius had left her water and bread, blanket and blade. Justinius had provided the comforts that anyone at home would have provided for a traveller. And he was to be her guard on the journey. She tried to catch the Praetorian's eye, but he had already turned to leave.

She ducked under the gates' wooden lintel as Bala moved into the arena. Fresh air at last—it smelt like nectar.

Crowds lined the route to the river, cheering and throwing palm leaves. Aoife rode Bala at the head of the parade of elephants, flanked by guards ready to use their spears if the elephant broke ranks. The onlookers fell back as she passed. Again there was the rapid movement of hands making the sign to ward off evil spirits. Some, caught by her gaze, looked instantly away; others stared, frozen, open-mouthed. When she had passed by, the crowd seeped forward again like a tide, to cheer the Emperor Claudius riding in his golden chariot. Behind the emperor came the inexorable tramp-tramp of marching soldiers, making their way to the boats which lined the river bank.

Rome. The city looked small, insignificant, as Aoife looked back from on board the raft she was riding with Bala. Slowly the great hub of the wheel of the Empire shrank and disappeared round a bend in the Tiber. Her spirit shook itself free like a bird. Great Rome was, after all, only buildings, dusty streets.

She released Bala's ear, which she had unconsciously gripped tightly from the moment the raft was cast off into the river. The oarsmen bent to their task and the raft swept into the current. Aoife caught her breath, exhilarated: Rome and four years of slavery were over.

A flotilla of deep-hulled transports waited for them at the port of Ostia. Atop Bala's shoulders Aoife watched the other slave-keepers haul their charges on board. The ships rocked as the elephants, each led by a slave-keeper, and prompted by the spear points of a dozen soldiers, scaled the gangplanks, two to each vessel. The quayside boomed with their baleful trumpeting.

Then it was their turn. 'Bala,' Aoife whispered, scratching behind Bala's right ear. Bala turned her head to show that she was listening. 'Get ready to move forward when I do this.' Aoife gently tugged Bala's ear. Bala rumbled to say she understood.

When they came to the gangplank, which was still swaying with the movement of the first elephant, Bala hesitated. She lifted her foot and held it above the planks forming a narrow bridge to the boat. She looked down at the choppy waves which splashed over it. Men, carrying spears, moved towards her. Aoife stepped first on to the gangplank, then, holding with one hand to the guide rope which spanned the gangplank from ship to shore, she turned back to give Bala's ear a gentle tug. 'Come,' she said. 'Now!'

Bala put her foot on the plank.

'Garn!' yelled a man, darting forward with his spear. As the weapon brushed her leg, Bala swept the man into the water with a lightning blow from her trunk. The gangplank lurched, threatening to throw her off. Aoife held on to the rope. 'Get back!' she said to the approaching soldiers. 'Don't threaten the elephant! She will board quietly if you stay back.' The soldiers paused, then lowered their spears. Again some made the sign.

In response, Aoife raised her hand and made her own sign over them. It was the sign of blessing, but the soldiers started back and raised their spears. Aoife stroked Bala until she was calm, then led her on to the ship.

It was a busy noisy place, a floating camp, where each man, woman, and animal was assigned their own quarters: the horses and elephants were housed in separate bays in the hold, more comfortable quarters than the deck open to all weathers. The store animals, goats, sheep, and chickens assigned to the cook, were housed there, in the open, facing whatever wind and wave threw at them.

Bala followed the first elephant down a ramp into the gloomy hold. At the bottom of the ramp, soldiers guided them with spears down a central gangway and then into their bays on either side. The first beast, already fearful, blundered off and almost ran into its quarters, butting the ship's side as the gate was closed behind it. The vessel rocked with a wild motion, setting off geese, goats, and chickens to call out with fear. Aoife waited for the ship to settle, then led Bala into the companion bay on the opposite side of the hold. A soldier watched her with wary eyes as she chained Bala to the wall, then latched the gate shut behind them.

The floor of the bay was covered with straw; otherwise the compartment was empty except for a water barrel.

Wooden walls divided it from the ramp area on one side and further bays, packed with bales and boxes, on the other.

Aoife looked into the barrel. There was some water but not enough for a voyage which, she knew, would take several days. She adjusted Bala's chain so that she could easily reach both water and hay, then stroked her flank. Bala stood calm, her eye pressed to a square porthole from where she could see the sea. 'You comfort me,' Aoife murmured. 'I'm afraid, but you are not.' What was Bala thinking? Her own mind was too disturbed, too clouded to hear Bala's thoughts.

'I have to find water. I'll be back,' she said, and received a quiet rumble in reply.

She went to the gate, unhooked the latch, then slipped out of the bay. As far as you could see down the ship, there were more gated bays and, at a distance of thirty paces, another ramp, down which a horse was being led, bating its head as it slipped on the slimy planks.

Past the ramp next to her bay, the hold broadened out into a place where bales of hay were stored, next to large tuns of water. It gurgled and slopped lazily over the sides with each sway of the ship. A slave in a loin cloth was filling a pail. 'We need water here!' Aoife called, but he did not look up or make any sign that he had heard. She walked forward and was prevented by the length of a spear, thrust across her chest.

'Halt!' A centurion emerged from the shadows. 'Get back to your bay! Wait your turn, witch!' Aoife's eyes flamed, but she obeyed.

Shortly after her return, someone threw a fresh bale of hay over the gate. It was heavy to lift, so Aoife dragged it towards Bala. As she did so, the straw covering of the bay floor, now disturbed, exuded a foul, acrid smell which she recognized from the voyage to Rome, when she had been a prisoner in the crowded slave hold. *Rats*.

Shuddering, oppressed by the memory of the rats which, without fear, had swarmed over sleeping bodies, searching out the dead and the dying, Aoife groaned and pushed her face to Bala's warm flank. Then she looked out from the hollow behind Bala's great knee, and scanned every crevice of the bay. She must find their holes—they were probably coming up from the bilges—and block them up. Rats were clever at hiding. Night time was their time for foraging.

A trumpet sounded. Slowly, with jerky movements, the ramps were drawn up and knocked into place with loud thumps. The hold was closed. 'We will survive this,' Aoife whispered, holding the edge of Bala's ear. 'We will.'

A trapdoor in the nearest ramp was flung open, and a rope ladder dropped through. A man poked his head into the hold. 'All slaves on deck,' he called. He glanced at Aoife. 'That means you!'

Aoife patted Bala's neck and left the bay. She climbed the ladder through the trapdoor to the next deck, where the oarsmen sat on wooden benches, then up to the top deck, where she found a place to stand, in the stern, with the other slaves, looking back at the shore. Eyes darted to her and moved, unsmiling, away. Some made the protection sign again, surreptitiously pointing their fingers. No one spoke.

The ship fell quiet as if holding its breath. It rocked slightly, waiting.

74

'You!' The man, from his dress the ship's captain, pointed his stick at her. Behind him, the men, sailors, and guards, stopped what they were doing, to watch.

'You! Witch! Stand away from those slaves! You'll spend the voyage below! Get her back to the hold!' A centurion stepped forward and poked his sword at her. Aoife was forced back to the trapdoor.

She sat, hunched, next to Bala and heard the distant shout of the steersman and the muffled beat of his drum. Long oars slid into the sea. Another shout and then came the first steady pull—slide, catch, and lift—as the oarsmen started to row.

A VISITOR

She couldn't sleep. While Bala stood, as if carved in stone, by the porthole, for hour upon hour, watching the repeated stroke of the oars, Aoife twisted and turned in her bed of straw, curling into a ball, head to knees, then on to her back, then on one side, then the other, her mind fraught with questions. *How long will they let me live? Ships have their own laws, I have no protector. Will they kill me? Not even the emperor can save me, if the captain decides to have me killed. They think I'm a witch! Where is Justinius?*

The trapdoor opened and the ladder dropped down. Footsteps approached the bay. *They were coming for her.* Aoife jumped up, and stood crouched, hands spread wide, ready to defend herself.

'Well met, Flavia.' Carpus Alexander unlatched the gate. The boy from the pen opposite scrambled up from his bed of straw to look at the prestigious visitor; with an urgent gesture, Aoife waved him away.

'You fought well in Rome to escape me, but you see I've caught up with you. The gods are on my side, after all: they know you are mine.'

Carpus stepped towards her. 'Stay back!' she warned.

'Stay back? Why? I'm your saviour. Why do you doubt that?'

The trader pushed past her to examine Bala. She snorted and lunged, threatening the trader with her tusks. 'Vicious beast!' he cried, shielding his face.

'She knows her enemies!'

Carpus patted the scar on his cheek from the wound made by the wolf. 'Still full of fire, sweet Flavia.'

'My name is Aoife.'

'By whatever name, after the emperor's triumph, you shall be my reward.'

'Never!' Aoife said.

With a vicious stroke, the trader knocked her to the ground, then caught and held her by her long hair.

'You listen to me. While you are on this ship, you are in danger. The captain carries no prisoners. If you offend him or his men, he will throw you overboard to be eaten by the leviathan.' Aoife struggled. 'Ha! I thought that might get your attention.'

He threw her aside. 'Believe me, Flavia, I am your only hope of surviving this journey. Your life is in my hands now.' Carpus pulled her to her feet and attempted to brush straw from her tunic. Aoife pushed his hand away. 'We must work together,' said Carpus. 'I have promised the captain that you will obey me. I've assured him that as long as you are kept here in isolation, your powers will be kept in check.'

'I have no magic! I'm not a witch!' Aoife moved away from the trader, and stood with her back to the hollow of Bala's flank.

'The elephant won't save you, my dear. Only me. *Witch . . . Druid . . .* by whatever name you choose to describe yourself, you cannot deny your gifts.' He pointed a threatening finger at her. 'But you must share them with no one else. There must be no exhibition of gifts on this journey. No healing, no charming of beasts, no chanting of spells. You are mine, and your gifts are mine, to use as I see fit.

'I was going to take you back to Rome, to have sole charge of my premises on the Street of Silent Knives, but it may suit us better to install you in one of my villas in Britannia—'

'You are a madman,' Aoife said.

'Ha! Not so mad, my dear. You realize that Claudius will have you thrown into the arena, after the triumph? He has promised the men—cowardly fools, every last one of them—that they shall see the Celtish witch die. It will be difficult to save you, Flavia, but not, I think, impossible. When all's done, you will thank me.'

'What of the elephant?' Aoife said. 'Will you save her?'

Carpus laughed and shook his head. 'They will hold the games. The beast will die in the arena.' He turned to leave. 'I shall see you in Gaul. Consider your position, Flavia. Live, on my terms, or die. It's your choice.'

As the trader climbed the rope ladder, Aoife leant against Bala's side. The elephant shifted her trunk backwards, to hold Aoife close across her chest. 'You shall not die in the arena,' Aoife murmured. 'You shall not.'

STORM

For several days the flotilla of twenty or more ships journeyed on, from Rome to Massilia, their port of destination on the southern coast of Gaul.

Aoife watched the other ships from the porthole, marvelling at the unvaried pattern of the oar stroke, so regular, so constant, ship matching ship; day or night, whenever she looked, it was the same.

For a large part of each day the ramps were lowered, admitting light and fresh air to the hold. Soldiers brought food and water for herself and for Bala, throwing it to her over the gate of the bay. They averted their eyes, but they did not speak to her and there was no more mention of witchcraft. Neither were there any further visits from Carpus Alexander. She was relieved about that, but sad not to see Justinius, whom she had relied on to come to her. Perhaps he was not, as she had thought, on board the same ship.

In spite of her fears, for herself and for Bala, she managed to sleep for part of every night, lulled by the rhythmic sound of the oars as they crossed a calm sea to Gaul. Then, one night, she was awakened by the urgent touch of Bala's trunk to her cheek.

She jumped up, to see a scurry of movement from the

corner of her eye. *Rats!* In twos and threes they were issuing from a narrow jagged hole in the floor of the bay, a mere two finger's width—rats could dislocate their bones when they chose and squeeze through the slenderest gap—and were now streaming purposefully across to the floor and under the gate.

'Tss!' The young boy called to her and pointed to the gangway. Aoife unhooked a swinging lamp and went to look. The line of rats was heading from her bay into the boy's, then climbing a hay bale to head out of the open porthole. The rats were leaving the ship. 'What does it mean?' asked the boy.

'I'm not sure,' Aoife replied. 'Loosen the chains on your elephant,' she said, more from instinct, than from any clear plan. 'Make her lie down.'

As she finished speaking, a lurch of the ship knocked her off balance, and, within the next quarter, she and the boy staggered like drunkards, as the sway of the ship increased to a heavy swell.

Aoife hurried back to her own bay and loosened Bala's chains. 'Lie down,' she said, pulling at Bala's ear, but Bala had her own plan, and remained where she stood, planted four square. Aoife gave up trying to persuade her and they stood together, by the porthole, watching the angry sea.

At first she was not alarmed. The ship was strong, a protecting cradle, that would easily ride the heavy waves. Then, as time went on and the storm broke with great crashes of thunder and forked lightning, the sea, like a boiling cauldron, threw the ship about as if it were driftwood. She shivered, hearing the fearful cry: 'Man overboard!' and the terrifying response: 'There's nothing to be done. Pull! Pull! Row for your lives!'

Aoife clung to Bala's chain. Torrents of water crashed through the porthole, drenching everything. When the ship lunged forward, like a hound released from the traps, she dragged Bala to the middle of the bay, so that she could close the porthole with a piece of wood, set there for the purpose.

Against the increasing roll of the ship, it took all her effort to secure it, but at last it was done. She banged the latch into place.

The boy shouted to her, a cry of alarm. She stumbled to the gate and saw him staring at her, as his elephant repeatedly banged its head against the wall of its bay. Aoife helped the boy to calm her, loosening her chain and encouraging her to lie down. Then she sat in the straw with the boy, with their backs to the elephant's side, and put her arm round his shaking shoulders.

The trapdoor was flung open and a rope ladder dropped into the hold. As lightning cracked across the sky, men with swords grabbed Aoife and forced her to climb the ladder. '*Watch Bala!*' she called to the boy.

All eyes were on her, as she came into the open. The storm beat down like a punishment. The ship groaned with the effort to stay afloat. Aoife's face streamed with rain, her hair plastered to her skull. Two guards, legs spread wide to keep their balance, held her, as she faced the ship's captain. The sails had long been furled. The bare masts stood stark against the sky, like threatening fingers. Those men left on deck stood to watch, their hands gripping ropes or steering gear, some still hoping to manage the ship, others hanging on for their lives. The captain spoke to her, but his words, which were, from the look on his face, full of anger and fear, were lost in the rush of the wind. She was pushed to the side of the ship. A priest stood there, his robes whipping his thin body. As he pointed at her, delivering his judgment, Aoife finally caught some of the words. 'Great Neptune . . . deliver us! Save us! We beseech you! We give you . . . the WITCH!'

As the guards prepared to thrust her over the gunwale, she heard someone scream: *'WAIT!'* and twisted to see Carpus Alexander arguing with the captain.

Iron hands held her shoulders as she stared down into the black waves. She tried to tell her captors about Bala, the emperor's elephant, but they wouldn't listen. Like a rotten carcass, she was hefted over the side of the ship and thrown into the tumult of the sea.

Roar of waves—so loud, so loud. Murky water in her eyes. How much longer could she hold breath? Long strips of seaweed whipped her face, threatened to strangle her. She tore them away. She was released.

She took in a breath and breathed air. She shook the sea from her eyes and saw the ship's prow rear up like a startled stallion, then plunge into the sea. Great Neptune had not listened to the sailors' prayers.

As the ship crashed into the water, the main mast snapped like dry kindling, and the ship keeled on to its starboard side. Men leapt from every part, every deck, every porthole, as the vessel cracked apart like a broken egg. *Where was Bala? Where was the boy?* Aoife's whole body clenched with dread, then a piece of flying debris hit her head and, unconscious, she fell backwards into the sea.

When she came to and opened her eyes, she was still in the water, her arms embracing a plank, her face pressed to the wood. The sun warmed her face. All around was a chaos of wreckage: spars and ropes, floating mats of dirty straw, jars and bowls, blankets, boxes, bales and chests, all bobbing about in the waves. And everywhere there were men, soldiers, sailors and slaves, some shouting to Great Neptune, or to Mithras, the soldiers' god. Some cried for their mothers, some flailed their arms in the water, others clung, without moving, to pieces of timber.

Horses. She saw a troop of them, swimming together, moving purposefully through the sea: they were heading for a hazy line on the horizon. Land.

She measured the distance. Could she swim? Using the plank, she must try. With trembling muscles, she flexed her legs and, pushing the plank ahead of her, set off for the land.

Something nudged her back. Too weak to turn and look, she knew only that she was being pushed forward.

Men stood on the shore in small groups, some staring back at the waves, some bending to pick up a piece of cloth or some object or other that had been washed up. One figure stood out, still in his purple robe, which hung limp and sodden, and clung to his body. The emperor lives, Aoife thought as something nudged her again. This time she managed to lift her head and turn to take a look.

Bala. Bala was pushing her along with his trunk. She

was swimming. Aoife dropped her face to the plank and laughed and hugged it as if it were the most precious thing she had ever seen. Bala was alive. She could swim. She looked back again. As Bala flapped her ears, Aoife caught sight of the boy, and the other elephants, all seven in a group, swimming as if born to the sea, all making for the shore.

There was something else. Dead bodies, floating face down in the water. *Don't look back. What's gone can't be mended. Look ahead.* The words inside her mind made her look again at the shore. Carpus Alexander was there, waving and pointing. He was speaking to the emperor.

In the smoky murk of a taverna on the beach, the soldiers avoided her. If they had to pass near, they fell silent and stepped up their pace. They blamed her, the witch, for the storm and the shipwreck. Given the chance she knew they would get rid of her now, before they took another step on their journey. But Roman soldiers had to obey orders, and the order to dispose of her was not given.

Someone threw a blanket around her shoulders. She twisted to see who it was and saw only the confused mass of legionaries on the other side of the room: loud, boisterous, laughing and drinking with the easy arrogance of the conquerors. There were Gaulish peasants, too, in sombre clothing, solemnly serving their masters with false smiles.

She pulled the blanket closely around her shoulders: whoever her benefactor was, the blanket was warm and welcome.

A soldier was preparing to throw dice: 'Felicitas! Good luck!' he cried, to the nods and winks of his compatriots. 'Those who *were* about to die, salute you!' He threw and the dice came to rest. A silent breath, then a cheer. He had won the throw. He grabbed the dice to try again and was prevented by someone laying a hand on his arm. The man, closely hooded, took up a great bronze cup and held it still as it was filled with wine. As he lifted it, his hood fell back. It was Carpus Alexander.

'Friends,' he said, 'I'm here to tell you that the storm was foretold. It was the work of Rome's enemies in the east who wished to depose the emperor. Hail, Claudius!' He drank from the cup and the room echoed with the toast, as the company repeated it. 'Hail, Claudius!'

Carpus wiped the back of his hand across his lips. 'The Celtish girl had no hand in it. You have no need to fear her. She is under my protection. Here! Another toast! To victory!' Again he lifted the cup. 'And to great Jupiter who has spared us!' he cried, then drank again.

He passed the cup to a young soldier and stood over him while he drained the remaining wine in one attempt. The dregs splashed on to his tunic, but he slammed the cup down and grinned widely to have passed the test, before turning away to vomit on to the tavern floor. Grimacing, amid laughter from the other soldiers, Carpus stepped back. A sour-faced Gaulish peasant girl came with brush and pail to clean up the mess.

Watched by the company, Carpus approached Aoife. 'Keep the blanket,' he said. Aoife instantly threw the blanket aside and stuck her frozen fingers under her armpits. Smirking, Carpus walked to the door.

'The elephant saved you,' whispered a familiar voice in her ear.

'Justinius!' All her fears fled like mist in the sun as he looked down at her.

'Sh—' he warned, sitting next to her. 'Do not sound so pleased to see me!' Aoife flushed, looking away to hide her smile as he briefly touched her hand. 'I thought I had lost you,' he said. They shared a look, confirming the bond that had sprung into life between them, but could not yet be put into words.

'I didn't know such beasts could swim,' Justinius said lightly, pouring wine for them both from a ewer. 'They are like giant seals.'

Around them, men stared, then at a sharp glance from Justinius, went back to their own conversation.

'It was the will of the Mother,' Aoife said. Justinius handed her the wine.

'I'm glad you survived,' he said.

'And the elephant?'

'Yes, that too.' His words warmed her, but in the chill when the door was opened, Aoife shivered.

'Put on the blanket,' said Justinius, placing it around her shoulders. 'Please,' he added, when she gripped it to throw it off. 'The cloth is innocent: it can't harm you, and whatever else, you must avoid arousing Carpus's anger. He is powerful and vindictive. The emperor listens to him. So far, your position has been secure, as keeper of the elephant, but the storm has not helped your case. The rumour persists that you have magic powers. There are those who will try to persuade Claudius to have you killed. Carpus Alexander is your only ally, and it is a long way to Britannia.' Justinius drained his cup, then stood up to leave. 'Regulus!' He called one of the guards to approach, an older man with a good-humoured face. 'Stay with the Celt, then when you have finished your supper, escort her to the night shelter.'

Before leaving, Justinius addressed the company. 'You men!' he said. 'This girl is a valuable British hostage. She has endured accusations of witchcraft and was thrown off her ship for it during the storm. The men responsible have been punished; their bodies float in the harbour. She is no witch! Think about this: if she did cast a spell, then it fell short of the mark, since we have all survived, including the emperor! What was lost? Two ships only, some slaves, some barrels of wine—sad losses, but hardly damaging to the invasion. Whatever powers she has are no match for the might of Rome!'

Amid cheers, he added, 'Drink well tonight, we leave at dawn,' then he caught up his cloak and left.

WAR ELEPHANT

It was still dark when Aoife heard Bala's cry. It pierced her mind like a sword, before she heard it piercing the wind. She scrambled out of her bed of straw, struggling to move her stiff limbs.

The quay was strewn with heaps of spoiled cargo, washed up by the tide. The debris caught at her feet as she made her way to the animal pens, where Bala was calling. When she arrived, a dreadful scene met her eyes.

Flames surged from makeshift forges: the air was thick with sparks and the smoke from charcoal fires. Gaulish slaves wielded their bellows. Smiths, with faces like polished bronze, hammered, blow after ringing blow, at pieces of red-hot metal.

Behind the forges, the elephants were held fast in chains. All stood, a little uneasy, still submissive, except one, whose shadow reared and plunged, as she fought her captors. Bucketing away from the fire, Bala struggled in a net of chains, held by twenty or so slaves.

'Let me through!' Aoife shouted. 'She's terrified!'

'Stay back, witch!' said a guard. He flicked his fingers and a burly soldier grabbed her and held her back.

'Keep it steady!' shouted a man, a bystander wearing a long dark cloak, with a high collar that hid his face. But

Aoife recognized the voice: the emperor supervised this task, whatever it was.

'*What are you doing to her!*' Aoife shouted to him.

Hisssssss . . . Dense steam pothered up as the smiths plunged their work into a vat of cold water. When they retrieved it and held it aloft in the claws of giant pincers, Aoife's breath caught in her throat. It was a mask, an iron mask, for Bala's face, a monstrous piece of armour, with holes for eyes, and side plates, to cover from brow to jaw.

'*Claudius!*' Aoife cried.

The emperor swung round and struck her. '*Do not dare speak my name!*'

'Caesar, if I may—' Justinius placed himself between them.

'*What is it?*'

'The slave thought the elephant was in danger. She does not understand what she sees—'

'I understand very well!' Aoife cried, pushing Justinius aside. 'You are turning her into a war machine, a weapon, one of your soldiers. You must not! She will not wear your armour!'

Giving her a look of contempt, Claudius gestured to the slaves holding Bala and they dragged at her head, so that the mask could be put in place.

'*Ba . . . laa!*' Aoife cried, a single cry, but it was enough. Bala's head jerked up. Guards with spears ran at her as she broke free of her chains. When the first man came within range, she jutted her tusk at his tunic and threw him across the quay. Then she roared and stamped her feet, and the smiths dropped their tools. The iron mask landed with a clang on the ground.

Aoife's guards relaxed their hold on her and she too shook herself free. She went straight to Bala, who, breathing heavily, turned to meet her.

Behind her, Claudius watched Bala bow her head and lift Aoife on to her back. Pushing past his own guards, he went to them, a red flush of fury creeping up his bare throat, as he glared up at Aoife. He shook his clenched fist at her.

'You overreach yourself, Celt!'

'Let me tend to the elephant!' Aoife shouted, over the barrier of spears, as the emperor's Praetorians rushed to protect him.

With an effort, Claudius controlled his fury. 'This beast is the one I must ride in my triumph. The soothsayer foretold it. This is the one! She must be protected with armour, as we ride through Gaul. This expedition is no holy day outing, Celt! With each step we move further from Rome and closer to our enemies.'

You are afraid. Aoife bit her lip to stop herself speaking the words out loud, as Claudius glowered up at her, then, whisking his cloak around himself, stalked away. Watching him leave, Aoife shuddered and pressed her hands hard into Bala's bristly hide. Claudius was unsettled, unsure. Confronting him was extremely dangerous. She must take more care in future.

'Very well, Celt! The beast will go without armour!' he shouted. 'Get her down and chain her,' he added. 'When we leave, she will march in chains.'

As the soldiers hurried to obey his orders, he swung back to Aoife: 'You will beg for death when we come face to face with Caratacus.'

* * *

Carpus Alexander came with the change of guard to the shelter where Aoife was being held. Her shackles were removed.

'You will not march in chains: Claudius sometimes makes very hasty decisions. I spoke to him, on your behalf, after he had calmed down somewhat. "How can the girl tend the beast if she is chained?" I said. "She is still your prisoner. You may still have her killed." He agreed. You will tend the elephant better without chains. Flavia, you were foolish to provoke him and you must not do so again.'

'He must not harm Bala.'

Rubbing her sore wrists, Aoife watched Carpus hawk-like, as, with an oily smile, he moved closer.

'Claudius washes his hands of you,' said the trader. 'He has turned you over to me. I have promised him your complete obedience from now on and you will be under close guard at all times. It was the best I could do.' As he put his hand over hers, Aoife snatched it away. 'Can't you raise one little smile for me, Flavia? You're mine now,' said Carpus.

THE FOG AT THE END OF
THE WORLD

To Aoife's relief, Carpus Alexander stayed away from her and Bala during the long days of the march, but as he had warned, the emperor sent two of his men to guard her. They took turns to dog her every move.

As the weeks rolled by on the journey from Massilia, where they were shipwrecked, to the port of Gesoriacum on the northern coast, she grew used to her guardians. The story of what had happened on the quay only added to her reputation as a witch, who had bewitched not only the emperor's elephant, but the emperor himself. Every day, some soldier or other came to taunt her, shouting out, 'Witch! What's the secret?' as if they had a wager on the answer. Sometimes they asked her about Bala. 'Does the elephant do tricks too? Make her sing! Make her dance!' A fierce stare was usually enough to deter them. Finally, they tired of the game and contented themselves with following her, making the protective sign against evil whenever she spoke.

She did not see Justinius. The days passed in the routine of tending to Bala, riding her or walking at her side. Marching calmly, without chains, the elephant seemed resigned to the task, but Aoife had not forgotten her vow. She would save Bala and, with the Mother's help, send her home.

Madoc haunted her mind, an ever-present pain. Where was he now? She thought of him in different places, and attempted to practise what Bevis had taught her, to avoid the heartache of 'what if—' and picture Madoc, instead, alive and well, among friends.

When she rode Bala, from her high perch she studied the soldiers about their business and understood why the legions carried all before them like an attack of locusts. Every man followed orders in a rigid pattern of activities: weapons practice, equipment inspections, recreation, discipline, punishment. At the heart of it all was the emperor's chariot, surrounded by a solid phalanx of Praetorian Guards. Aoife stayed well away from Claudius, keeping Bala close to the other elephants. The boy from the wrecked ship, who had also survived, travelled with her.

The weather grew colder as they moved north. One day when a thunderstorm threatened, the order was given to break out thick cloaks, one for each legionary. Aoife looked at the clouds and knew that the storm would pass. Summer at home was always like this: shine and showers.

Justinius came to bring her a cloak and some soldiers' socks to wear. He stood by the entrance into the animal pen and placed his gifts on the fence.

'I can't stay,' he said. 'Don't come any closer. It's for the best.'

'It's good to see you,' Aoife said. Rumbling a greeting, Bala went up to him. He patted her cheek.

'Do you have news of Madoc?' Aoife said. Justinius shook his head, rubbing Bala's hide, while Aoife bent to bundle up hay, tears pushing at the back of her eyes.

'There'll be more chance of news when we get to the

coast,' he said. 'I'll keep my ear to the ground. If there's news to be had, I'll find it.'

'What will happen to me when we get to Britannia?' she said.

Justinius paused then said, 'I shall take you to your tribe.'

'My tribe? The tribe of Edain?' She had not dared to hope that any of her people had survived.

'Yes. They are gathering a force to join Caradoc's army.'

She dropped the hay and went to the fence. 'My sister Igren?'

'I don't know, I'm sorry.'

Justinius paused, then said, 'We have to tread carefully. A word could betray us.' He smiled and Aoife longed to cross the distance between them. Then, as he turned away, she lingered by the fence, watching the swing of his red cloak as he marched down the path.

'Handsome lad, that.' Carpus Alexander walked towards her, his voice as smooth as cream. 'Taken a fancy to him, have you?'

Without reply, Aoife went back to her task and Carpus watched. The silence unnerved her. She wished he would leave or speak. But he stayed until she left the pen to go back to her tent, and followed her, watching until she lifted the flap to go inside, then he left, still without saying a word.

It took another six days to reach Gesoriacum, during which she saw no sign of Carpus or Justinius. As the emperor's company joined the rest of the legions from across Northern Gaul, who were still encamped there, Aoife took Bala to explore the terrain. Her spirit rose at the smell of brine on the wind. It was so different from the smell of the Great Sea, the Roman sea, which they had crossed from Rome to Gaul. It was the smell of home.

As soon as she could, she went to stand on the shore. Across this mass of grey water, a short stretch away, lay Britannia. Narrowing her eyes, she strained to see past the misty horizon; her heart pounded and swelled, as if to burst from her chest. At last she was going home. It was a dream; it was not real; she would not believe it until she could see with her own eyes and stand on the soil of home.

She sought permission to take Bala back there, for longer every day, to the top of the cliffs, to fresh pasture. Her request was granted, though she must take a small detachment of guards with her, armed with torches and spears, in case of incident.

There was a place where the land was scooped out, forming a grassy hollow, an old quarry perhaps. While Bala grazed there, watched warily by the guards, Aoife climbed alone to the clifftop, to look out at the sea.

The opposite coast, curtained in thick grey mist, kept its secret. The soldiers had a name for Britannia: '*The land at the back of the north wind.*' They believed that it stood at the very edge of the world, where the spirits of the damned wandered in a dense fog, bereft and forlorn, forbidden, for their sins, from ever entering the afterlife. Old hands scared new recruits with their stories: *The spirits of the fog feed on the unwary! And if you escape their clutches, don't forget to look out for the world's end, or you might fall off and be lost for ever!*

The loud crack of distant ballistas firing practice shots from the plain behind took her attention. The engineers rehearsed an attack.

Aoife surveyed the camp: hundreds of grey linen tents set out in lines, within squares marked out by fences of sharpened stakes. From the clifftop they resembled counters on a games board. The restless masses of horses, penned in their corrals, moved like dark stains.

The troops practised their manoeuvres, turned with precise movements—*Halt! Attack!*—with a great shout, thrust forward their swords again and again—jab, retire, jab—keeping their faces protected behind rectangular shields.

Aoife hugged herself as cold fear closed on her like an iron fist. This was invasion—*no holy day outing*. Most of the legions had already crossed to Britannia. Claudius would cross only when the battle was nearly over and he was certain of victory. At this very moment, her people were fighting for their lives. They would fight with passion, giving body and soul, blood and courage, to their leader, Caratacus, whole families fighting together. It would not be enough.

The men on the plain below, immeasurable numbers, were not even the chief invasion force. They were a second army, kept in reserve. Four legions, 25,000 men, had already invaded. The truth was as clear and cold as blind justice. It was a matter of logic. Caratacus would fail.

She turned her back on the plain and looked at the sea. Fog was rolling towards her. Soon it would envelop them, camp and all. Britannia lay behind its curtain. Its shroud. She threw up her arms and cried to the sky:

'What can I do? Mother, show me!'

An answer came. *Fight, though it cost you your life. Fight, to your last breath, for what is most dear to you.*

'You! Celt! Stop that!' A rough shout drew her attention to the quarry. Bala rumbled a threat as the man drew a sword and made to climb up to Aoife.

'I'm coming down,' Aoife said.

As she returned to the hollow, more men, carrying firebrands, came into view. Carpus Alexander led them, stabbing a long spear into the ground as he laboured up the slope.

He directed two men to hold Aoife, while others surrounded Bala, who growled and bucked away from them. Though Bala fought them as well as she could, with her legs in chains, they forced her back into the scooped out wall of the hollow. Men with torches closed in and kept her at bay, while others bound her securely with strong ropes.

Keeping his distance, Carpus flourished his spear at Bala, like a scholar, with a pointing stick, teaching a lesson, then he stopped and indicated the powerful sinew that stretched, haunch to knee, down her back leg.

'What are you doing?' Aoife cried, struggling with her captors.

With a powerful jerk, Bala tossed her head. Men shouted with alarm, but they had learned what to do, giving a little slack on the rope, then snatching it back again, until Bala's head was forced to the ground. Carpus leant on the spear, resting his cheek against the blade.

'I will not risk taking this beast further on this expedition, without a simple precaution.'

'What precaution?' Aoife cried.

Carpus's men forced Aoife back to the lip of the hollow. The trader came to speak to her.

'Claudius will ride this beast into the stronghold. As he does not have your powers, it must be tamed to obey him, in the usual manner.'

'What are you talking about?'

'Why bother yourself with such a trivial matter? My dear Flavia, when Claudius rides in triumph, you will be long gone to my villa in the west.' From the hollow, Bala roared with distress. Aoife sprang forward, but Carpus prevented her. 'A small cut to the hamstring,' he said. 'Soon over, soon forgotten.' He flicked his fingers and a giant of a man appeared, carrying an axe.

Bala reared, flailing feet and tusks, as Carpus's men strained to hold her. The giant prepared to deliver the blow.

Glancing aside, Aoife caught the flash of a red cloak. *Justinius.* The Praetorian, with a dozen soldiers, came into the quarry.

'What is this? Let go of the hostage!' he said. Carpus shrugged, then let Aoife go. Resisting the impulse to run to Justinius, Aoife walked slowly across the quarry, to stand next to him.

'Carpus Alexander!' Justinius called. 'Why do you threaten the emperor's elephant?'

With insolent slowness, Carpus moved his head to address him, as if he had not seen the Praetorian arrive. 'Justinius! What brings you here?' He looked from Justinius to Aoife and back again, then he held up his

hand. 'No matter. I shall answer your somewhat imperti-
nent question, if only to reassure you that I act only in
the emperor's own interests. As do you, I'm sure.'

He paused, then waved towards Bala: 'See how the
creature bucks and rears! It must be tamed.'

'Do you have the emperor's permission for this proced-
ure?'

'Go back to your duties, Justinius,' said Carpus, with a
sneer, 'and leave me to do my job.' He clicked his fingers:
the giant lifted his axe. Aoife's mind raced. He must not
hurt Bala. As the man polished the axe blade on his sleeve,
she pushed away from Justinius and sprinted to the top
of the cliff.

Standing on the very edge of the quarry, she looked
down, then stretched out her hands, making passes over
the scene below, as if performing a spell. Pointing her fingers, she made the horned sign against evil. Drawing his
sword, Justinius started up the slope.

'Come no further!' she cried, pointing the sign at him.
He hesitated and pushed out his hand to stop the soldiers
following, as thick mist rolled around Aoife's shoulders.
'Stay back! I'll deal with her!' he called.

Aoife threw her arms wide and her head back. *I call
down the Mother's anger on all who harm this beast,'* she said,
giving her voice as much authority as she could. *'Fall on
them, fog at the end of the world. Fall on them! Draw them to
confusion!'*

The soldiers stared at her. Some stepped back.

'Cover them, lead them to destruction!' Aoife called. *'Let the
spirits take them and feed on them, until they themselves are
mere wraiths, left to wander the mists of your realm for ever!'*

A soldier on sentry duty on the brow of the hill yelped, dropped his spear, and fled. One by one, others followed.

Seeing the soldiers fleeing, Carpus's men also ran. 'Stay where you are! It's a trick!' Carpus ordered, but they fought each other to get away from the cliff, then ran, dropping torches in their wake. 'I'll have you flogged!' Carpus cried.

'Send doubt and despair! Take them into your vast region of nothingness. Let none escape!'

As the folds of mist crept past Aoife towards them, the rest of the soldiers wheeled away from the hollow and ran down the hill. Justinius sheathed his sword.

One by one, the men holding Bala peeled away, and, as the fog approached, the last one, the giant, lumbered after his comrades, leaving Bala swaying in a tangle of ropes.

Carpus reeled like a spinning top and bellowed after them: 'I'll see you in Hades for this!'

Aoife pushed past Justinius and went to free Bala. Carpus came to her, swimming out of the mist like a spirit himself, as she untangled the ropes.

'My own Celtish witch—what a performance!' he murmured. Justinius arrived at the foot of the slope. 'What a show from our hostage, was it not?' Carpus chortled.

'What happened to your men?' said Justinius.

'What happened to yours? Call themselves soldiers? Pah!' Carpus spat.

'They were all southern-born, trader, keen to see the northern sea they must cross. I brought them here to see for themselves that the voyage will be a simple matter. Instead—well—they have shamed themselves. You should not have attacked the elephant, then the Celt would not have put on this ridiculous show—'

Carpus was shaking his head. 'Did I not witness a strange event here, Justinius? Why did you not seize the girl when you had the opportunity and prevent this—*show*? Did the hostage befuddle your mind too, with her spells?'

Justinius gave a snort of disgust and started off down the hill. 'On your life, do no harm to the hostage. Deliver her and the elephant safely back to the camp or we shall all suffer the emperor's wrath,' he called over his shoulder.

Carpus's eyes narrowed as he watched Justinius leave. He turned on Aoife and wagged his finger at her.

'Very well, Flavia, have it your way for the time being. But know this—I shall tame the beast for the emperor's triumph, one way or another.'

THE EMPEROR'S PLANS

The next day, in the camp, Aoife waited for the emperor to send for her. He must know the story, of how the Druid's daughter had routed his men by commanding the fog to come. Had she gone too far?

As she walked from her tent to the animal pens, as she led Bala to the stream and set her to graze in the meadow, the soldiers fell silent as she passed, keeping a distance. Some averted their eyes, some made signs to ward off magic. Aoife was pleased that the all-powerful Romans seemed less sure of themselves. She feared for her life and longed to speak to Justinius: she could not die without knowing that he had forgiven her for the trick.

She was shovelling dung into an ash pit when a guard came for her. She was summoned into the emperor's presence. Shaking, she washed her hands, then wiped them down her tunic and brushed her fingers through her hair. The guard's expression revealed nothing. He pointed his spear down the track to the emperor's tent. Aoife ducked out of the pen and followed him.

Claudius lay at his breakfast, with Justinius standing, impassively, at his side. Attendants stood behind the emperor's couch, one holding a plate piled high with fruit, the other holding a large jug. Claudius was eating figs. As Aoife was pushed into his presence, he held up a gold cup, into which the slave at his shoulder poured red wine. He stared at Aoife, drank the wine in one swallow then sat up. A slave hurried forward to attend to the folds of his robe and when the emperor was satisfied, backed away, head and shoulders bowed. Full of dread, Aoife managed to straighten her own shoulders and lift her chin to watch him.

A soldier entered and, with a brisk salute, stamped to attention. He held out a scroll of papyrus to the emperor.

'Justinius—' The emperor's gesture was clear. Justinius took the scroll.

'It's a message from Aulus Plautius, Caesar. The route across the Med Way river is secure; the British in retreat across the Thames. The legions are in pursuit.'

Claudius sat up. 'Casualties?'

'Eighty-two men killed, forty-four wounded. All safely shipped back to port and now being cared for in the infirmaries.'

'Fetch me my armour!' he called to the guard by the door. 'When is the next tide?'

'Just after sunset,' called a voice from the shadows. Carpus Alexander stepped forward, offering a chart to the emperor.

Claudius waved the chart away. 'Yes, yes. I take your word.' He turned back to Justinius. 'Prisoners?'

Justinius scanned the scroll. 'The southern tribes have all surrendered. The general has ordered the construction of forts to maintain order in the territory. The troops will await your arrival, north of the river Thames.'

'And Caratacus?'

'In hiding. Some say he had fled to his western strong-hold.'

Claudius stood up. 'I must have him,' he said quietly. He looked angrily at the door. 'Armour! Bring me my armour! Why do you not obey me?' Two slaves hurried in bearing the emperor's war gear and began to dress him.

'Why are you still here, Carpus? Attend the beasts.'

Carpus Alexander bowed his head and left.

'What other news?' Claudius signalled Justinius to continue reading the scroll.

'There is mention of the hostage's brother. His ship was attacked, in a night assault. The boy jumped overboard and was picked up by a sole vessel—no identifying marks—after which it made its way northwards. The report is that the boy lives.' Aoife gasped, her cheeks flushed with joy. Claudius made no comment on this when he next spoke to her.

'I am told that you bewitched Justinius. How did you do that?'

Aoife's joy faded. Fear pressed on her, as if she were inside a shrinking cage, but she faced the emperor, unflinching, biting her lips together, while she considered how best to reply. She didn't have to. The emperor suddenly swung away to address Justinius.

'Perhaps you can explain, Justinius—' Claudius spoke quietly at first, but as he went on his voice rose to a terrible shout, *'how a Celtish slave cast a spell on my soldiers, so that they fled like spineless cowards!'*

'Caesar!' Justinius sprang to attention. 'She cast no spell! It was a trick! The men should have held their positions. I take sole responsibility. They were under my command—'

'Under no command but the *girl's* is what I heard! *What were you doing on the hill?*'

'I was doing my duty. Some of the southerners fear the crossing. There are many stories told about the "land at the back of the north wind", superstitions I had hoped to quash by showing the men the sea and the coast beyond. When I reached the top of the hill, I found Carpus Alexander there, with the hostage and the emperor's elephant. The trader was about to harm the elephant, and the girl did what she could to stop him.'

Justinius waited for the emperor to respond. Instead Claudius merely said coldly, 'Go on.'

'I do not trust Carpus Alexander. I believe he has his own plans for the girl.'

'Does he indeed?' Claudius stared at Justinius with eyes like stones. 'Carpus has told me that you want her,' he murmured. Justinius fell silent.

Aoife looked steadily ahead, keeping her eyes still, her fingernail cutting into her fists. *Why doesn't he speak?* she thought. *His silence incriminates him.*

'He's wrong, Caesar. I have no use for her. She's a burden and a hindrance to me. Although I itch to be rid of her, I have believed to this point that she was best kept alive. That is still my opinion. Now the brother lives to become the next leader of the tribe of Edain, who will no doubt move to strengthen the rebel army, we must keep the girl alive to draw him out. I am certain he'll attempt to rescue her.' Justinius spoke with measured calm, his clear eyes fixed on Claudius's face. 'My first duty has been to safeguard the hostage and the elephant, in preparation for your triumph. Now it must be to capture the brother, then we can kill them both and rout their tribe before it recovers from such a blow.

'To that end, nothing must prevent the girl's safe arrival in Britannia, and with your permission, I shall double my efforts from now on.'

Justinius clicked his heels to attention. Claudius reached for his cup as the candle flame burnt and flickered away the minutes. Taking a sip of wine, he studied Aoife.

'I could have you killed *today*, *now*, this *minute*—' He gave a signal—'Justinius!' There was the sharp hiss of metal as the Praetorian drew his sword. Moving with slick expertise, Justinius held her from behind with his sword at her throat. She felt the rasp of his chin on her cheek. He made no sign to her, but stared straight at his emperor, but the blade did not touch her skin. Justinius did not touch her with his sword.

'Wait!' Aoife said. 'Listen to your Praetorian! My brother *will* come for me!'

Claudius motioned Justinius to stand down.

'I believe he will. Justinius's plan is a good one. You may thank him for your life.'

He seemed calm now, but his eyes flickered briefly, between her and Justinius. Aoife jolted with fear: *He's watching us. He knows.*

Claudius sat back on his couch. 'I'm curious, Celt. You have put seeds of doubt into the minds of rational men. Are you truly a witch? You command the elephant. Can you also command the weather and call down wraiths?'

'I cannot,' Aoife said. *Not by myself. It is the Mother who works through me.*

'You make no claim to have magic powers?'

'Certainly not.' *Edain's power is not the magic of soothsayers and conjurers.*

'Then what happened on the clifftop? The men claim that you summoned the eternal fog at the end of the world. They say it came at your bidding.'

Aoife laughed nervously. 'It was only a trick to distract Carpus Alexander. They were hurting Bala. I saw the mist rolling in and used it.'

'Bala?' Claudius put down his cup and fixed her with a sharp look. *Had she made a mistake?*

'It is the name of the elephant.'

'The beast has no name.' The emperor leaned forward. 'So far, Celt, I have been lenient, but let us clearly understand one another. For the time being, Justinius has convinced me to spare your life. But you must be punished. The men must see that you have no power over me.

'You have enjoyed certain privileges of free speech and movement, not usually allotted to a prisoner: those privileges are now at an end. You will continue to tend the elephant—' He broke off, then called out for his scribe. A slave entered, clutching a tablet and stylus to his chest. 'Make a note,' said Claudius. 'The Imperial elephant. After the triumph, it is to be sent to the arena with the others—'

'*No-o-o!*' Aoife lurched forward. Justinius held her back.

'—an apt gift to the gods,' said Claudius, as if she had not spoken, 'in cognizance of the part they have played in delivering our victory. Is that clear?' The slave finished writing and nodded. 'Dismissed,' said Claudius. The slave retired.

'You must not kill her! You can't!' Aoife locked eyes with the emperor.

'*Can't?*' With surprising speed he crossed the distance between them and put his hand to her throat, lifting her until she stood on the tips of her toes. 'You cross me for the last time, Celt. One more word—' His fingers tightened viciously, stifling her breath. 'Soon you will stand on your native soil again, and I shall set watch for your brother. Meanwhile, if you make any attempt to escape— if I even suspect you of it—I shall not wait, I shall kill the elephant at once.' He let her go.

'*What about the prophecy?*' Aoife cried.

Already leaving, Claudius laughed. 'It is the mark of an emperor to disregard prophecies,' he said. He called to his guards. 'She is no witch. Release her,' he said. 'She will cause no more trouble.'

GALEN

Justinius caught up with her as she wandered along the harbour. He reined in his horse and leaned down to speak to her.

'I think Claudius suspects something. You must be ready to move. I'll come for you.' Before she could question him, he had hitched up his reins and cantered on.

Ready to move. She was not ready. She could not abandon Bala. The harbour at Gesoriacum was her prison. Claudius had read her mind with the skill of a seer, knowing what would bind her; the cost of her freedom, Bala's life, was too high to pay.

The emperor's men still dogged her steps, but when, after an hour or so, they were diverted to take wine and play dice with a group of soldiers squatting near one of the barges, she climbed the headland alone.

She loved to look out at the sea. Already the first ships were setting out. Trumpets sounded and the drumbeats from the hands of a hundred steersmen pounded like the heartbeats of gods, as more vessels edged slowly into the channel. Aoife caught her fists to her chest, as a wave of fear took her breath and her strength away. Thousands of men were crossing the sea to Britannia, to reinforce the thousands already fighting there. If all the tribes fought together, every last man, woman, and child, they would be too few against such a force.

A freak gust of wind carried the sound of horses, like a call from home. In the next bay, a man shouted orders and others replied. She leapt over clumps of rough sea grass to the edge of the cliff and threw herself down to take a look.

In the bay, hidden from the main harbour, horses milled in a noisy group. They were being herded on to Roman transports. Four men drove them down a wide track to the beach. The leader sat on his horse apart, watching them from the top of a mound. He wore Celtish clothing: plaid breeches and a blue cloak, thrown over one shoulder. His black hair, long and loose, was wiry with dust, as were his drooping moustache and beard.

The horses clambered on board; the noise of their hooves was like thunder on the wooden planks. Men shouted numbers and made marks on tally sticks.

Aoife breathed in the smell of horses, the smell of home. Before she could stop herself she had scuthered down a sandy track into the bay. She would speak to the man: she would speak her own language again.

'Galen! Well met!' Justinius rode past her to greet the trader.

'Huw! You've been promoted!' the man replied. 'Are you now the emperor's purse?'

Justinius laughed. 'I've brought payment for this consignment, and orders for a further two hundred horses, if you can deliver them, within the month.' The trader went to question one of his men and Justinius spoke to Aoife. 'You are putting us all at risk. Go back to the harbour, now.'

'Who's this?' Galen called, in Celtish, as he returned.

'A British Celt,' Aoife said in her native tongue. The smells and sounds of home impelled her to speak to the trader. She pushed back her hair to reveal her brand.

'The mark of Edain. The sign of Bevis,' Galen said slowly. He narrowed his eyes.

With a shrug, Justinius glanced at Aoife. 'Trust him,' he muttered, then turned away. 'I'll keep watch.' He urged his horse up the slope.

'You are blood kin of the Druid Bevis?' Galen said.

'I'm his daughter, Caradoc's sister's child.'

'*Aoife*,' Galen said, bowing his head. 'We had word of your coming—'

'Is there news of Madoc? Or my sister Igren?'

'No news of Igren, I'm sorry.' She blinked away tears. 'Surely Madoc is with you?' Galen said.

Aoife shook her head. 'We were separated in Rome, then there was a report that his ship was lost, but he was saved by an unknown vessel. I had hoped to hear news of his reaching Britannia.'

'Wherever he is, Mother keep him,' said Galen. 'Your brother's return will breathe new life into the tribe of Edain. Yours also.'

'My return? You speak as if I were free to join them. What can I do? I'm still a prisoner!'

Galen fell silent for a breath, then said: 'Rome holds much of the south-east; Caradoc is desperate for help.'

'Don't say so!'

'I could take you home now, on this tide,' Galen said. 'Come with me.' Aoife's stomach clenched, as she took in what Galen was saying. If there was no news of Madoc, if

115

he had not survived—if her brother was dead—in Galen's eyes she was the next leader. How could she step into that role? She was not ready. And she could not abandon Bala. She had vowed to save her—*a life for a life*—and to send her home.

'I can't!' Aoife shook her head. 'Justinius would be blamed—'

'My men will present Justinius with your bloody tunic, saying you threw yourself from the cliff and dashed out your brains on the rocks. They managed to salvage the tunic, but a powerful current won the battle for your poor remains. Justinius will report your death to the emperor and show him the evidence.'

'*No!*' Aoife said.

'*Why not?* It's a clear chance to escape—I don't understand!'

In the angry silence between them, Aoife struggled to find the right words. How could she lead the tribe? What if she were the last of her family left alive, the only one with a blood claim to lead her people? Then her duty was clear; she must do as Galen asked. It fell to her, as the Mother willed. Edain had brought her here, to this meeting, she knew it. Yet she must keep her vow. She must keep her promise to Bala. She took a deep breath, then said, 'Take my word to the tribe that I shall come to them, as soon as I am able to. They must prepare for war, they must gather weapons and supplies—'

'They know those things better than you! They are ready now! It's you or your brother they need to see, in the flesh, to prove that the Mother has answered their prayers! Can't you see what it would mean? That Rome was not able to keep you prisoner. That we can defeat the invaders and thwart their purpose, that—'

'Galen, enough. I cannot do what you ask, not yet. I have a vow to fulfil. A life depends on it.'

Angrily, Galen turned his back to her.

'These are fine horses,' Aoife said, in a shaky voice, as his silence continued. The last few animals were being herded on to the ships. 'You supply horses for the emperor?' Aoife said. 'Why do you sell such beautiful creatures to Rome?' She longed to go to them, to run her hand along a flank, and mesh her fingers in a coarse mane.

Galen turned back to her and held out his left arm. The inner flesh was deeply scarred from elbow to wrist. 'My arm is useless: I cannot lead a tribe! I do what I can. I'm a trader, and, under cover of commerce, I carry messages for Caradoc, along the coast of Gaul.'

'You're a spy—'

'A messenger, one link in a chain.'

'That stretches from Britannia to Rome—Damianus, Justinius—'

Galen gave a rapid shake of his head and looked around, as if they might have been overheard. Aoife took the hint and changed tack.

'These are not like British horses,' she said. 'Their legs are longer, their heads held high.'

'They are my own,' said Galen, relaxing, dropping his shoulders, 'bred from Moorish stock, fast and strong.'

'They present more flesh to a sword than our stocky ponies.'

'These horses will not see battle: they have been ordered for the emperor's triumph.'

A shout from the boats drew Galen's attention. He stood up, shaded his eyes, then raised his arm to acknowledge the signal. The ships were ready to leave.

Justinius rode back from the harbour. 'We must hurry. You are needed to take the elephant on to the ship.'

'Elephant?' said Galen.

'You know these creatures?' Aoife said.

'Such magnificent beasts! They are not like any other I have had to deal with. They are almost human, seeming to understand every word you speak. A family with an elephant has a lifelong and loyal friend, with the strength of twenty men. An elephant can clear forest to make a place for a homestead, knock down the trees and drag them away by itself.' He looked at Aoife. 'You travel with an elephant?'

'Claudius has brought them from Rome. There is a special one, picked out by his soothsayer, which he plans to ride into Caradoc's stronghold. I am its keeper.'

'This is madness!' Galen said.

'You will see this madness for yourself, when Claudius lands his elephants in Britannia!' said Justinius.

'I shall not be there to see it. Within the week I head south, to Africa.'

'*Africa?*' Aoife pricked her ears. Galen's men, holding fast to the anchor ropes, called to him.

'I must go,' he said. 'We'll meet again, daughter of Bevis.'

'Galen. My elephant—'Aoife began, as a wild dangerous idea took root in her mind. 'I want—'

'Anything—'

'I want to return—' As she struggled to put her plan

into words, doubt assailed her. She had no means of paying Galen to take Bala back to Africa, even if he agreed that it was possible. And would it be right to take her back? How would she find her home again? Where would Galen take her in Africa? If he left her with the traders, they would simply put her up for sale again and she could end up back in Rome.

'You want to return? To *Rome*?'

On the clifftop a mounted Praetorian appeared and stood watching.

'Aoife—' Justinius murmured. He nudged her with his horse on to the path.

As he spoke to the Praetorian on the clifftop, Aoife called after Galen: 'Do you know a man called Carpus Alexander?'

Galen stopped. 'Do you?'

Aoife nodded.

'Steer clear of that one, my lady,' he replied. 'He's trouble.'

BRITANNIA

Eighty vessels of the emperor's fleet, decorated with a profusion of purple pennants, made the crossing to Britannia. The ship on which Aoife travelled with Bala was identical to the one on which they had crossed the Great Sea. With Bala safe in her bay, Aoife stood on deck to watch, as she approached the coast of home.

There was no fog to prevent their landing. The helmsman directed Aoife's ship into a cove, a little apart from the others, where a fort, now assigned to the emperor as his headquarters, had already been established.

Aoife steadied herself with one hand on the gunwale and the other on one of the ropes, and looked up at the watchtowers. Rome's flags and banners flapped there in a stiff breeze, like the wings of imprisoned birds, struggling to fly free. Her skin flushed and pricked. She was home, yet still a prisoner, under enemy power. She gripped the side of the transport as it swayed in the tide. Should she have abandoned Bala and escaped as Galen urged her to? Did Justinius have a plan? *I shall take you to your tribe.* Was it fair to ask him to risk his life?

She glanced at the open trapdoor and knew she must keep her vow: she must get Bala back to Africa.

'*It can't be done. You are helpless. You will be killed. Bala will die.* She countered her doubts with words she had learned at her father's knee: *'If a task speaks to your heart, no matter how great, you must make the attempt of it.'*

She would do it. Only then, after keeping her promise, would she be free to join her tribe, but she would need Galen's help.

Foolishly, as the ship butted the harbour wall, she looked for him among the teeming crowds on the shore. There were too many bodies, too many faces from which to pick out Galen's. Perhaps Justinius would know where to find him.

The gangplank was dropped into position and a line of soldiers streamed ashore, some still buttoning their tunics, donning helmets. Those given orders to guard the vessel set up a temporary camp on the sand, making pyramids of their spears, shouldering shovels and running off to dig the latrines or hack out firepits over which to broil their scant rations of corn.

A massed fanfare sounded as the emperor's own ship moved slowly to port. He himself was standing in the prow, clad all in purple with a gold wreath on his brow. He was throwing bay leaves into the water, as a gift to the gods for safe passage. Two priests on the shore wrestled a goat to the ground, ready to make sacrifice. As the goat gave up its life, there was a hush among the assembled troops, then a rousing cheer as the priest declared the signs propitious for the success of the emperor's campaign.

Claudius stepped off his boat and, flanked by guards, began to move up the track to the fort. A bonfire flared up on the shore. Men gathered around it. Someone began to sing.

'*You!*'

Aoife turned to the abrupt call. Stern-faced, Justinius ordered her ashore. As she stepped on to the gangplank, he stood next to her, then, out of sight of the others, pressed her arm and muttered: 'Come, set your foot on British soil again. You've come home.'

With shaking legs, she stood on the sand. It didn't feel like coming home. She tried to smile and failed, her mouth trembling. 'I'm not home yet. I'm still a prisoner.'

'That will change,' Justinius said. It was all he said then, and afterwards Aoife tried to recall the exact expression on his face, to read his true meaning.

'Prepare to disembark!' he called to the others in a loud voice, signalling a group of slaves on to the gangplank.

'What about the elephant?' Aoife said, touching his arm.

'It will be penned with the rest,' said Carpus Alexander, appearing from behind Justinius's shoulder. He looked from one face to the other, then drew his cloak round him, hiding his arms in its folds, as the wind blew his black hair across his brow.

'You will stay with the other keepers,' he said to Aoife, ignoring Justinius.

That night Claudius ordered a flood of wine in celebration of their arrival. The windy shore crept with the rolling bodies of drunken legionaries. In despair, Aoife watched them from the hollow in the sand under the transport's wide prow, where she was ordered to sleep with the other slaves, after long hours of scouring the hold and the animal pens. *If only Caradoc were here now. With only a small detachment we could sabotage the whole fleet. Then I could rescue Bala and the other elephants and ask Galen to save them all.*

As dawn mist wreathed the shore, Justinius woke Aoife and the other keepers to hear the emperor's orders. They were to prepare the beasts for the journey. There would be difficult terrain with marshes and a battlefield to cross, as well as two major rivers. They were to ensure that the beasts were well fed and watered every day and kept clean and free from disease. If the omens were right and their progress was unimpeded, they would make their triumphant entry into the rebel stronghold within the week. From now on they would ride the beasts at all times.

Stone faced, the keepers listened to their orders. None of them seemed concerned, and why should they be? The elephants were seasoned pack animals, used to being ridden.

Aoife wondered if Bala would allow it. Those few brief times when she had sat astride her had been at Bala's choosing. For most of the journey across Gaul she had walked at her side. To ride her was to show that she was Bala's master, something she could not say. She had not ridden her as the other keepers had ridden their beasts, with whips and sharp sticks to govern them.

It would be a useful rehearsal for the triumph, Justinius was saying, when, according to Claudius's orders, they would enter Camulodunum in strict formation: first would be the emperor's elephant.

The dark figure of Carpus Alexander appeared out of

124

the mist. He dropped a heavy sack on to the sand and bent to untie the neck, then tipped the bag over and shook out the contents.

'Some of you have seen these before,' he said, picking up a hammer and an iron spike. 'You know how to use them.' One or two of the keepers nodded. 'If you do not know how to use them, then find out.' He mimed the action of hitting the head of the chisel with the hammer.

'It can be done with a single blow, between skull and backbone. Familiarize yourselves with the exact spot for the strike, should the need arise. You must strike well, because you will not get a second chance. Each of you will carry these,' he said, emphasizing the point by holding the tools high. 'Use them only in case of strict need: for example, if the emperor's life were in danger, or if your beast should break ranks. If I find that you have killed your beast without need, your life will be forfeit and *you* will entertain us, instead of your elephant, in the games.'

He pointed to the bag, then to Justinius: 'Carry on.'

As Carpus left, Justinius handed out the tools.

'I shall not carry such things,' Aoife said.

'You must do as the others do,' Justinius replied, pressing tools into her hands, 'until the time is right.' Reluctantly, she took the hammer and chisel. 'Attend to your beasts!' he said out loud, then, without a backward glance, grabbed the empty sack and marched off up the track to the camp.

To Aoife's surprise, Bala stood in line with the other elephants and let her climb on her back, as the other keepers mounted their charges, without difficulty. *We will survive*, she whispered to Bala, as they rode inland with the rest of the emperor's retinue. Bala must go back to Africa and she must join her tribe. Two ambitions, which grew more hopeless as they journeyed on without opposition. There was no sign of Caradoc's forces, no sign of Madoc coming to her rescue. The dread thought grew at the back of her mind that Claudius's triumph would go ahead exactly as he planned. They would march, like this, to the stronghold, then Claudius would have her killed, and Bala would die in the games. *I shall not have saved her or myself.*

Without complaint, Bala plodded onwards. From her high perch, on Bala's back, Aoife surveyed the ravaged countryside. Where there would perhaps have been crops to harvest there was now blackened land. Wells had been spoilt, shelters ruined. Wild boar and deer, any creature which would have provided meat for the invaders, had been slaughtered. Their fly-encrusted bodies had been left in rivers and ponds, wherever the enemy might want to water their horses.

In some settlements they were welcomed by the supporters of the traitor Verica. Aoife's stomach turned with disgust as Celtish nobles bowed to the emperor's convoy. When that happened, she kept her eyes on the horizon and the threads of smoke, that, she told herself, rose from fires set by fighters loyal to Caradoc, burning all behind them as they fled from the coast.

The conquerors were not set back by the burnt fields and spoiled wells: they carried their own provisions and found stockpiles of grain and fresh water, left for them by the legions who had preceded them.

They came to the Med Way, to the site of the most recent battle. They heard it first: the sound of a million flies, feeding on the waste of the battlefield. Then came the smell. Aoife covered her nose and mouth as she and Bala crossed the river. She kept them covered until they stopped to make their next camp, deep in the next stretch of forest, beyond which was the road north to the Thames.

It was a hot night. Aoife led Bala to a glade a little way from the rest, then tried to sleep. It wouldn't come. Her mind was full of the sights she had seen, of the broken remains of dead soldiers. There had been no Romans among them. Their bodies must have been claimed by their comrades and taken away for honourable burial. Only dead and dying Celts had been left, to lie there, dishonoured. As her father had been left, four years ago.

They were near Aoife's home. It was almost unrecognizable, yet she knew it was the territory of Bevis. She was approaching it from an unfamiliar direction, yet it spoke to her. If only she could find a sign, some landmark, a rock, a stream, something. Heavy sadness choked her. Could she face seeing the grove again, where her father had died?

Bala rumbled and shifted her great bulk. To calm her and to soothe herself, Aoife got up and gathered a bundle of hay, using it to make long strokes along Bala's great flank.

Something moved among the bushes. Justinius appeared.

'All well here, Celt?' he said out loud, searching the bushes on every side with his eyes to make sure he was not observed speaking to Aoife. He crossed the glade, then made a show of examining Bala's legs for scars. 'Galen wants to see you,' he muttered, bending close to Aoife.

'Galen's here?'

'A mile to the west, there's a grove.'

I know. As if the goddess had opened her mind, with a painful stab, she remembered.

'Follow the path.'

I know the path.

'Go now. I'll guard the elephant.' Justinius patted Bala's flank.

'I'll be back,' Aoife said to Bala. 'Justinius will stay with you.' Bala rumbled quietly and touched Justinius with her trunk. Swallowing hard, Aoife smiled at them, then set off down the path.

IN THE GROVE OF EDAIN

Aoife approached the grove, on fire with memories, and stopped on the edge of a hill to look down at the place where the village had been. Moonlight lit up the empty plain. There was nothing left, no sign to show the settlement had ever existed, only a slight dip in the land, crescent-shaped, where the ditch had been. To the west was a glint of silver, the stream where Madoc had pushed his doll, Fenn, into the muddy bank. Four years had grown over it; the banks thick with rushes.

Holding back tears, she turned back to the path. She must not give in to grief: there was work to do. She walked on to her father's grove.

Edain's sigil appeared everywhere, carved into tree trunk and stone, long since covered by moss and dense ivy.

Voices came to her from the past, images loomed then faded: of a girl, her younger self, biting a soldier's hand as he carried her away; of Igren with her bloody sword shouting 'Run! Run!'; of Madoc, with big eyes and white face.

When the path opened out into the clearing she stopped. One step more and she would see the hut. Did her father still lie there on the threshold? *'Go on . . . go on.'* The voice in her head was insistent.

She walked into the circle of grass. There was no hut, no bones. Instead, a feeling of welcome. Home-coming. Figures in white robes walked with her. They wore wreaths of oak leaves on their heads and carried leafy branches. They sang and swayed to an ancient tune. They danced in the sacred grove, held in the circle of the Mother's arms.

She knew the song, though she struggled to remember the words. She heard the rapid pounding of horses' hooves and looked for them among the dark trees on either side, the wild horses of Edain.

A cold breeze made her shiver. The vision faded. There were no horses, no voices, only an awareness of them on the edge of her senses: she could still reach them, if she folded her mind to do so.

The outer circle, where her father's hut had stood, was a clearing of rough grass, kept short by the grazing of deer, hare, or wild boar. It was still cropped. The wild ones had not deserted the grove.

The edge was marked by large stones, each at a distance of ten paces from its neighbour, all chest high, except for the four marker stones marking north, south, east, and west, which towered above the rest. In the centre of the clearing was a dense group of trees, guarding the inner grove, where the most secret rituals were performed, and signs examined to divine the Mother's will and which paths the tribe should follow. Only the high priest might enter. At its sacred heart was a stone-lined pit, which fell deep into the earth and was positioned to receive the light of full moon, at summer's height, to shine straight down into its darkness. *The Well of Souls*.

Sometimes, those who had lost their way, felons or traitors, were sent to the Mother, down the Well of Souls. Bevis had kept her from the sight of such events, but she had once spied on the ritual, peering through a gap in the trees, curious to see what happened to one of the felons who was marched into the grove, but did not come out again. She saw it all and wished she had not. The cries of the condemned man, as he fell, still haunted her. The Well of Souls led straight to the Otherworld, the Mother's realm, from which there was no return.

By the entrance to the inner grove, stood the altar, a slab of stone, measuring a man's length and as wide as he could reach with arms spread. There Bevis would kneel, in full view, to speak to the goddess, laying his hands on the stone.

Bevis. Aoife was deep in her memories when a low whistle caught her attention. Galen stood watching her, next to one of the stones.

Instinctively Aoife laid both hands on the altar stone, as she had seen her father do countless times, seeking the Mother's mind. The stone felt cold and damp to her fingers, but she had to smile: she was taller and older since she had last attempted this. Now it was easy to place her hands on the altar. *I'm no longer a child*, she thought.

Galen came to her. 'My lady.' He bowed his head.

'The Mother be with you,' she said, in ritual greeting. She touched Galen lightly on his right shoulder, then on his left.

'And with you,' he replied.

'Why did you send for me?' Aoife said, quaking inside, because she had already guessed the reason.

'You were so close; your people wished to see you,' Galen said. Reaching behind the stone, he pulled out an old black staff, its head wrapped in a dirty cloth. He thrust the staff at her and she looked at it, as if it were an enemy's weapon.

'The tribes are gathering, eager to act,' Galen said. 'Lord Caradoc will avenge his brother's death—'

'Togodumnus is *dead*?'

'Yes. He fell at the battle of the Med Way. Many good fighters were lost—' Galen hesitated, not daring to speak on.

Her skin pricked. 'What is it?' she said. He didn't answer but moved away, as the grove silently filled with people. They crept out of the wood, laid their weapons, in untidy piles, outside the circle of stones and came forward, as more followed.

Men, women, children, dressed in rags, their faces thin and drawn from fear and starvation, came to see Aoife. As if she had been away for only a day or two, she knew them. She knew them all, and she rocked, thrown off balance, as if in a high tide. *Madoc? Igren? My sister Igren?* There was no sign of them. No sign of any of those people she had grown up with: Eluned, Addan, Seith . . . Sinnoch, Maxen—*where was her playmate, Helyn? Where was grandfather Gower, with his talking bird? Where was—?*

The ache of understanding clouded her mind. She locked the knowledge away, the grief, until she could bring it out again and face what the war had done.

'Your people,' Galen murmured. One by one the members of the tribe made the sign of the Mother, then fell to their knees. Galen peeled the cloth from the head of the staff, then raised it high. 'She has come back! The daughter of Bevis has returned!'

Amid shouts of celebration, Aoife held up faltering hands. 'I can't lead you—' she said. 'Justinius waits for me. I have to go back—'

'No. Justinius knows what story to tell. That you ran off, to join your tribe, which is the truth!' Galen led her to the altar. 'You put your hands on the sacred stone. I saw you. Your blood knew its destiny.'

'Don't ask me to do this! Madoc is my father's heir.'

'But he is not here. Aoife, this is the Mother's will.'

Again Aoife put her hands on the altar stone. She bowed her head.

'Ask the Mother,' Galen said urgently. 'Ask Edain what you should do.'

A clear whinnying cry broke across the grove. As if it were a sign from Edain herself, a horse trotted out of the wood. Justinius followed, limping.

'She threw me! She's never done that before,' he said, straightening his legionary's helmet. 'One minute we were riding quietly along the trail, then she reared up, as if stabbed, and bolted straight to this place.'

He planted himself in front of Aoife. 'I took the elephant back to the camp. You need not return; I've already warned the emperor that you might make a run for it, especially here, in your father's territory. Aoife, you must take this chance!' he said urgently. 'Caradoc has moved west: the stronghold is already in Roman hands and the tribes are surrendering, for a few sacks of grain. You are worth nothing to Claudius now. If you go back, he'll have you killed.'

Aoife stared at him. 'What about Bala?' Of course, not knowing of her vow, Justinius misunderstood.

'She was quite calm when I left her. I'll get another keeper, that boy you're so fond of, to take care of her.'

Leave Bala to her fate? Lead the tribe? Join Caradoc? Was this really the Mother's will? Quaking, Aoife moved to the entrance of the sacred grove and looked inside. There stood the pit, in thick shadow, the Well of Souls, the entrance to the country of the dead.

I need a sign, Aoife breathed. At her back, the people crowded as closely as they dared to the sacred place.

Aoife took a hesitant step through the entrance. As Galen whispered, 'It's your destiny,' she walked to the Well of Souls.

She stared down into the darkness, the dense heart of the Well, and the air outside became lighter. She looked up. She could see through the wood on the opposite side. It seemed to her that there were people gathered there, stretching back among the trees, as far as she could see, all of them watching, silently waiting. Her father was there and a beautiful woman with red hair, who smiled at her and lifted her arms. Was it her mother who blessed her? Behind her was grandfather Gower, his talking bird on his arm. *Lead them west. Save their lives.* Her father's voice came to her clearly.

So be it, she said. The shadowy figures faded. Between parted clouds, the first beam of moonlight pierced the gloom like a spear, striking the dark heart of the well. As Bevis had done before her, Aoife lifted her hands, palms upwards to the moon. *Mother . . . Guardian of Souls . . . Into your hands.* She turned and went back to the entrance.

'In the name of Edain!' she shouted and the roar of a hundred voices echoed her cry. 'In the name of Edain! In the name of Edain! In the name of Edain!'

Torchlight sprang up among the crowd. Galen gave Bevis's staff to Aoife. She touched the rectangle of pale wood just below the head of the staff, where she had prised off the emblem. She pressed home the splinters. There was a rustling among the crowd as something was passed hand to hand. A small boy carried the leather pouch to Galen.

'Aoife, there's news,' Galen said, watching her face.

He opened the pouch and drew out the bronze mark of Edain.

'Where did you get that?' Aoife said harshly.

'At the Med Way.'

'But Madoc carried it! I gave it to him.' She snatched the badge and examined it. Surely it was a poor copy of the badge she had given to Madoc? She touched the corner with the broken spike. It was not a copy.

Galen signalled one of the tribe to come forward. 'You found this?' The man nodded. 'Did you plunder a body for it?'

Aoife pushed past Galen to question the man. 'A boy with red hair, and the mark of Edain on his neck?'

The man lifted uncertain eyes to look at her. 'The dead lay piled together, covered in mud. They were all Roman, I swear it! I plundered no Celtish body!'

He covered his face. 'The lad did have red hair. He wore a Roman tunic! I did not recognize him!' He thrust forward, pushing his face into theirs. 'I picked up the pouch because I thought that it carried gold. I uncovered the Mark, and gave thanks that it had come into my hands. Mother blight my life if I lie! I didn't know it was Madoc. I didn't—'

The man dropped to his knees and sobbed into his hands.

Aoife witnessed his grief and listened to his desperate plea, as if from a distance. *'I didn't know! I didn't—how could I?'*

Madoc was dead. The words dropped into her mind like clear cold water drops, repeating themselves because they were not understood. Madoc was dead. He must be: he would never have surrendered the Mark, he would have died to protect it.

A flash of pure burning anger made her tremble. All her prayers, all her thoughts sent to bless him, had not kept him safe. She gazed past the man into the wood, which swayed and bleared. She had seen the dead. *Why did you not let me see Madoc?* she asked. There was no answer. The goddess stayed silent.

A weakness ran through her and she staggered. Justinius caught her and took her to sit on one of the low stones.

Galen addressed the tribe. 'We have lost Madoc, son of Bevis, Mother rest and preserve his soul!' A deep sigh ran through the crowd. All eyes were on him as he spoke. 'But the Mother is kind. She takes away, but she also gives. She has sent his sister, Aoife, to lead you.'

He tried to break Aoife's mood of stunned apathy, to usher her away from the grove, to gather her into the crowd, the tribe who were ready to welcome her home.

'No!' she said, pulling herself roughly away. 'I'm going

back!' She pushed the sigil into the pouch and thrust it into her belt.

'What are you doing? This is madness,' said Justinius.

'I shall make Rome pay for the death of my brother—'

'Galen has risked everything to set up this meeting. You must go with the tribe.'

Stricken, Aoife looked at him with wide eyes. *I shall avenge Madoc—*

'Then give me the Mark!' Galen said.

'No. It stays with me, my talisman—'

Galen held up his hand in warning, as something shifted among the trees. They all listened, holding their breath, and heard nothing except the plip-plop of leaves falling, one by one, signalling an early end to summer.

With an urgent gesture, Galen directed the tribe to leave. Before melting into the trees with the others, he threw Aoife a last look. 'The Mother protect you,' he said. 'For the sake of our freedom, act quickly.' Then he was gone. Taking a deep breath, Aoife stared at the place where he had entered the anonymity of the wood, then she and Justinius left the grove.

'I can't promise a second chance—' said Justinius, as Aoife hurried away from him on to the path leading back to the camp.

'You can't promise her anything!' Carpus Alexander stepped from the trees. A dozen soldiers followed him. Aoife and Justinius were seized and held.

'What's this?' he said. 'A tryst? Or an assembly of rebels led by a traitor?' He did not wait for an answer, but pushed past them into the grove. Scuffing his toe at the remnants of a meal, a small piece of bread and some chewed leaves, he bent to pick up the end of a bunch of blackened reeds. 'Still warm,' he said, giving Justinius a sharp glance. 'Men were here, with food and torches.'

He picked up a short strip of plaid cloth, unwound from someone's foot. 'We must report this to the emperor.'

Carpus walked into the inner grove. Aoife saw him lean over the edge of the Well of Souls.

'Permission to search the woods, sir!' barked the leader of the detachment, drawing his sword.

'Don't waste your effort.' Brushing dirt from his fingers, Carpus came back to them. 'We have the ringleaders here. Take them back to the camp. The emperor will be pleased with this night's work. Get them there alive and there'll be a bonus in it for you. Now move!'

Aoife managed to take one look at Justinius, before she was dragged away. The soldiers bound his wrists together behind his back. He did not struggle, but stared calmly at the ground.

'GIVE ME THE GIRL'

'Justinius . . . ' Claudius's voice could scarcely be heard, then he crashed his fist to the table, as if to smash it.

It was dawn the next day. Stripped of his insignia and dressed in a slave's grimy tunic, Justinius stood to attention at Aoife's side, in the emperor's quarters. His head was bare and dishevelled, his face livid with bruises. He had been beaten.

When Aoife glanced at him, briefly his eyes gleamed at her with a clear message. *Say nothing.*

Aoife heard Claudius say: 'Justinius, I cannot save you.'

The emperor addressed his audience of senators and the rest of his Praetorian guard.

'This man has betrayed me,' he said, in the ringing tones of an orator. 'He has plotted against me with the rebels. What should his punishment be?'

'The sentence is death,' said Carpus Alexander.

One of the senators leapt to his feet. 'This man is a Praetorian Guard. You cannot kill him!' Claudius fixed him with a piercing stare.

'He was indeed a Praetorian. Until three years ago, this man had an unblemished military record. His father Erian, a local chieftain from central Gaul, was an ally and friend to Rome. His son entered our service when he was twelve years old. His father wanted him to be a legate. Isn't that so, Justinius?' Justinius looked at Claudius but made no reply.

'The wishes of father and son do not always—' Claudius tapped his fingers together, *'coincide*. In the light of my nephew Caligula's eccentric behaviour, Justinius's own loyalties began to surface.'

'How do you know this?' exclaimed the senator.

'It was over a statue, wasn't it, Justinius?'

Again Justinius didn't reply.

'Some figure of a woman riding a horse, wasn't it? Some Celtish idol, their horse goddess, Edain. Caligula urinated over it and your father had the temerity to object, didn't he? What did Caligula do to him?'

Justinius's face was impassive.

'I'll tell you. He had him stripped, tied to a chariot and dragged behind it, not only until he was dead, but until his flesh rotted and stank and had to be burned on the refuse dump. Is that not so, Justinius?' Claudius did not wait for an answer. 'Senators, you may be sure that I watched the son carefully after the father's shameful death. *Keep your enemy close to you!* It's a useful adage. As soon as I became emperor, I promoted this man to my own Praetorian Guard.' Amid mutterings from the audience, the objecting senator resumed his seat.

'I should have predicted this: blood has its own set of rules. Now he has betrayed me, forging links with his own kind. He will die, and it is unfortunate for him that we are in enemy territory, because we must make an example of him, to the rebels, as a warning to others. His death will be slow and painful.'

Claudius looked directly at Aoife. 'The judgment is death by crucifixion, at the third hour tomorrow.' Aoife's breath left her body. 'Tie him to a cross. Hoist him up high, facing west. The rebels will observe what happens to traitors. Now, get him out of my sight!'

Aoife swayed. *Crucifixion.* Justinius would be tied to a wooden cross, raised on high, and left to hang, for hours or days, until his lungs were crushed by the weight of his body and his breath stopped. A scream welled in her chest. She bit her lip to stop it bursting out of her.

As Justinius was taken away, he did not look at her, but kept his eyes on some fixed point, straight ahead.

She was to blame. He had tried to save her and failed. If she had not wasted so much time in the grove. If she had gone with the tribe straightaway. *If only—* She sagged between her captors as despair opened all wounds, new and old. Her father, Madoc, Igren, and the others. Now Justinius. She was to blame. Inside her the demon laughed: *Look at you. Helpless again. Edain has abandoned you.*

Carpus Alexander was grinning and smirking and rubbing his hands. This was his doing. Aoife pushed back her shoulders against her captors' hands. *I'm still alive. Edain lives in me. You will not win me, trader.* She lifted her head and stood up. *I'm still alive and so is Justinius. We are not dead yet.*

The emperor poured himself a cup of wine and drank it in a single draught. He wiped his mouth with the back of his hand, then he turned to Aoife.

'You shall watch your friend die. It may take some time.'

'Caesar—' Carpus Alexander came to join Aoife.

'What is it?'

'Give me the girl. Justinius is the real traitor. I doubt she even knew these rebels. The elephant has proved difficult. We still need her.'

This drew Claudius's attention.

'The elephant. Yes!' He stabbed the scroll. 'Plautius tells me that the tribes have surrendered the stronghold and Caratacus has indeed fled to the west. Nothing stands in our way! We shall enter the stronghold as conquerors; as *gods*, I should say!' He drained his cup. '*I* shall ride the elephant myself from now on.' He gestured to a guard to take Aoife away.

'Caesar, give me the girl,' Carpus said, without missing a beat. 'Allow me to choose the method of her death. Enter her in the victory games, as a gift to great Jupiter. Allow me to pit her against beast or gladiator.' He rubbed his scar. 'She fights well.'

Claudius broke into a smile, then clapped his hands. 'So be it! She shall fight—yes! Pit her against a bear, or a—what is it?—a baan shee! You are divinely inspired, Carpus! Prepare something interesting!'

Aoife was held overnight in a prison tent, next to the infirmary, where soldiers sick with infections or rheumy fevers lay groaning or calling through long dark hours for their mothers or sweethearts. At dawn the doctor had arrived. The men had fallen quiet then. She heard them answering the doctor's questions, with clipped responses, as if from a distance, her thoughts full of Justinius. *At the third hour* . . . in the morning, then, only a few hours after dawn. There was not much time. She prayed for his deliverance.

A lone soldier had been assigned to watch her and take her to the site of the execution at the appointed time. Her guard sat on his haunches, dozing, in the corner of the tent, his spear leaning against his knee.

Aoife rubbed fatigue from her eyes. Her thoughts wound on like tangled thread. *Galen. If Galen knew of their arrest he would surely attempt a rescue. If only Galen were here. Surely he had heard by now. Surely he would come.*

After a meal of dry bread and water, the guard left the tent to relieve himself. As the tent flap closed, Aoife heard someone scratch on the canvas then, a breath or two later, the flap was pushed aside. Galen entered.

'I thought he'd never leave. I was about to come in here and persuade him!' Aoife hugged him, then let him go.

'Where's Justinius being held?' said Galen.

'I don't know. They're going to crucify him—'

'Shh . . . don't concern yourself, they will not kill Justinius.' He lifted the tent flap and peered out.

'You'll be caught—'

'No. We traders are above suspicion, free to move about the camp. Don't worry, everything's ready.' He smiled at her. 'When the execution begins, there will be a diversion, so keep a sharp look out, because your people will come for you too. The emperor will expect us to take you both to the woods, but you'll head for the estuary. I have ships there. You'll board one of them and travel north.' A man coughed outside the tent and Galen stood up to leave.

'Galen—' Aoife struggled to move the words past the tight knot in her throat. 'There's something I must do. I made a vow— I can't abandon her—' Aoife's fear broke her voice.

'The elephant.' He nodded, as if he had been expecting Aoife's request. 'I've seen the way you handle her. You have a bond with her.'

'You've watched me?'

'Carpus Alexander is an old and dangerous rival. When you mentioned him on the beach at Gesoriacum, I made it my business to watch over you.'

'I never saw you watching—'

Galen smiled and looked away, and she knew that he prided himself on his ability to observe without being seen.

'The elephant carries a scar between the domes of her brow?' He chopped his hand to the middle of his forehead.

'Yes!'

Galen nodded thoughtfully. 'I know her. Her owners will be glad to see her again.' Aoife smiled. Was it possible that Galen knew the very place that Bala had come from?

'Africa is a hot land, isn't it? With palm trees and red dust?' she asked. *A young boy calling at the end of a very hot day. Dark-skinned, shading his eyes. A farmyard scudding with clouds of red dust. A barn roofed with palm.*

'The elephant was taken from a farm near the city of

144

Carthage.' He lifted the tent flap and peered out. 'Stay alert. It will happen very quickly,' he said, on the point of leaving. 'I'll do my best to rescue the elephant, but you must get her down to the estuary.' Looking back at her, Galen added, in a serious tone, 'I shall not risk lives to save her.'

BALA

Shortly after Galen left, Aoife was summoned to Bala's enclosure.

'*Salve*, Celt.' Claudius put his hand on one of the tripods of strong stakes with which the enclosure was made secure. 'I shall ride the beast,' he said. 'Show me the trick of it.'

Bala waited in a far corner, rocking steadily backwards and forwards with a monotonous chink of the chains binding her feet.

'You must take off her chains,' Aoife said.

'I shall not. The beast is still wild,' said Claudius. There was a surprising look of fear on his face, then his eyes narrowed and, through gritted teeth, he said, 'Wild or not, it will carry me, or feel my displeasure.' He seized a spear from one of the guards. 'Open the gate!'

A soldier opened the entrance to the enclosure.

'Attend me, Celt,' said Claudius.

Full of disquiet, Aoife followed him into the pen. Bala faced them head-on as they approached. Soldiers gathered along the sides of the enclosure. 'Remove the chains!' Claudius gave the order. Slaves sprinted to do his bidding, as he walked boldly up to the elephant. When Bala was free, she trod ground, stamping her forelegs into the dirt.

'Go no further!' Aoife called. 'Let me speak to her!'

'Nonsense,' said Claudius, advancing. Bala growled an obvious warning, then lowered her head to look the emperor straight in the eye.

'You're scaring her!' Aoife called.

'This creature shall know its master!' said Claudius. He brandished the spear. As Bala's warning growl increased in intensity, he roared at her: '*On your knees, beast!*'

Within reach of the slashing spear, Bala quailed, jerking away from the stinging blade. Slowly she bent her knee and Claudius looked triumphantly at Aoife. '*Kneel!*' he roared. '*Kneel!*' Bala did not kneel. At the next stab of his spear, she took a step backwards and began to curl up her trunk.

'*She's preparing to charge! Get out of the way!*' Aoife called, as Bala prodded her tusks forward. Bala's eyes blazed: she was too angry to be calmed now. Aoife ran to the gate of the pen.

'*Kneel!*' Claudius's shouted command turned to a shriek as Bala charged. Twisting away, he stumbled and fell into her path. At once a host of Praetorians leapt the fence. Two helped Claudius to his feet, escorting him to safety, while the others drove Bala back with their firebrands. One lashed her across the face with his whip, again and again. She reared and lunged, and knocked him aside.

The order was given to retreat. The men left the pen, closing the gate hurriedly behind them. Bala threw herself again and again at the barrier, trumpeting her rage. The stakes held.

Finally she calmed and stood in the centre of the pen, head down, her great body trembling. Aoife clung to the gate and called to her quietly, 'Bala. Bala.' The elephant raised her head briefly to look at Aoife, then lowered it again, her trunk trailing in the dust.

Carpus Alexander's iron fingers gripped Aoife's arm. He took her to where Claudius sat, catching his breath, a little distance from the enclosure. A slave wiped the emperor's hands with a perfumed cloth.

'That animal is still wild!' said Claudius, addressing Carpus. 'You promised me obedience! Tame it! Or kill it!'

'As you wish!' was Carpus's curt reply.

'What will you do to her?' Aoife said, before being taken away by the emperor's guards.

'We shall dig a pit,' Carpus said, signalling two of the soldiers to follow him.

BALA AND THE PIT

A pit was prepared inside the enclosure: twice a man's height, four times as long, four times as wide, with a steep slope at one end. There was a single entrance at the top of the slope.

Seated between her guards, Aoife watched Bala brought to it. Driven by men with torches Bala blinked with the sting of the flames and the acrid smoke. She was hobbled with fetters front and back. Men dragged her forward with ropes.

At first Bala fought them, throwing her head back, forcing them to use all their strength to hold her, but the cord, tied across her mouth, was so tight that it cut into the corners, and she roared in pain with each toss of her head. Step by step, she was forced to the edge of the pit.

As she came to the brink, the fetters were removed and the ropes dropped. Suddenly free, Bala stumbled in her own forward momentum and fell down the slope. Aoife leapt up and called to her. A soldier silenced her with a blow from his spear.

Standing at the bottom of the pit, Bala lifted her trunk and roared, shifting her feet in an attempt to climb back up the slope.

Carpus Alexander gave orders for the guards to stay

away from the pit and watch the elephant from a distance. 'Leave it to learn that it cannot escape!'

'Stop this! Stop it now!' Aoife cried.

'And condemn the beast? *Tame it or kill it.* You heard the emperor. Is that what you want?'

A soldier brought wine and bread, and bent to speak to him.

'We are summoned to take our seats for the execution,' Carpus said.

'They said the third hour—' Aoife cried.

Carpus looked up at the sun, a pale ball hidden behind thin grey cloud. 'We shall be gone by then. Reports have come from the Thames. We must march there today, to meet the generals. Claudius will not risk a delay.' He looked down the long alley which led to the open ground at the other end of the camp. It was a flat area of cropped grassland, where the soldiers practised manoeuvres. They had turned it into a small arena, where they held contests; single combat between two warriors, or between hounds, or between dogs and wild creatures they had trapped in the woods.

'I don't know why they've sent for us, in such a hurry,' Carpus said, 'when the site is not even ready—'

Aoife stared to where he pointed with his piece of bread to the arena, where men were now struggling to position a great piece of timber. Using ropes they hauled on it—*'Pull! Pull! Pull!'* shouted the centurion—then, with a sudden jump, the timber crashed, upright, into the hole they had dug for it. Aoife shivered with cold fear. *It was Justinius's cross.*

Carpus chewed his bread. He tore off a piece and

offered it to Aoife. 'We have plenty of time to deal with the elephant, as well as time to finish our breakfast. Join me, my dear—'

Aoife refused the bread. She felt sick. Loud cheers erupted from the practice ground. A throng of people poured into the arena: soldiers, slaves, smiths, cooks, senators—everyone in the camp came to witness Justinius's execution. As they took their seats, jugglers, mimes, and minstrels criss-crossed the arena, to entertain them with their tricks.

Carpus stood up. 'Look bright, Flavia, for heaven's sake: I despise pallor. Come, I am ready to face the beast!'

Dragging her eyes away from the arena, Aoife followed Carpus to the pit.

'I shall always call you Flavia, it was my mother's name. When we are married, if you prefer, when we are alone, I could call you *Eeva*, outlandish name that it is, but only if you please me.' The trader hummed with quiet contentment. Aoife's mind filled with an impenetrable fog.

'Within the month, Claudius returns to Rome,' Carpus said, 'and I have orders for new triumphs. I have purchased new animals: bears, wolves, nothing unusual. The trader Galen will transport them. He has ships in the estuary. Do you know him?' Dark-eyed, Aoife stared at him. Was this a trick?

In the pit, Bala roared piteously, swaying to and fro at the foot of the slope. Looking down at Bala, Aoife controlled her panic and gathered her thoughts. She knew what to do.

Behind the enclosure was the pen where the horses

were, and behind that, the track leading through marsh-
land to the estuary. At this hour, there were few soldiers
about: everyone, guard and slave alike, was hurrying to
the arena. Only a token force stayed with Carpus, to deal
with the emperor's elephant, and they made it clear, with
constant glances towards the arena, where they would
rather be.

If Aoife could get Bala out of the pit, she could ride her
round to the horse pens, as if practising the stately walk
required for the emperor's procession. When she came to
the track into the marsh, she would prompt Bala to race
down it, to the estuary. None of them knew how fast Bala
could run. Aoife had guessed at it and she was sure no
one would be able to stop her.

She was excited and scared: her heart felt too big for
her chest. She and Bala would be killed if the attempt
failed, but she had to try. She put on a smile as she spoke
to Carpus, but avoided looking into his eyes.

'Carpus,' she began. The trader froze, shocked by her
friendly use of his name. 'You must allow me to deal with
this elephant in my own way. I shall persuade her to
carry the emperor.' *Mother forgive the lie*. 'Look at her—
she's distressed and afraid. A frightened animal will lash
out. You don't want that to happen when the emperor
rides her into the stronghold, do you?' She forced
herself to touch Carpus's hand. 'Let me charm her for
you. I have a spell which will render her submissive
for the rest of the expedition. The emperor will think he
rides on clouds.' She pressed his hand with her cold
fingers.

Carpus looked at her with calf's eyes. 'Flavia. My

Flavia. You will teach me these tricks when we are married—' he said.

'Of course,' Aoife lied.

Aoife sat in a corner of the pit, feeding Bala handfuls of hay. On her instruction, a slave brought a pail of fresh water. As Bala took a deep drink, Aoife laid a hand on her face. 'It's all right. It's all right. Don't be scared.' She repeated the words like a charm, to calm her own fear.

Finally, Bala was ready and Aoife prepared to lead her out of the pit. The soldiers had laid wattle mats on the slope, to cover the smooth clay soil and allow Bala some purchase for the climb. Aoife tapped Bala's trunk, preparing to move her to the foot of the slope, then she jolted with fear as a blazing torch, thrown from the edge of the pit, struck her shoulder.

Choking, she wiped ash from her eyes. Carpus stood above her, his face like stone. 'Come out of the pit,' he said. Aoife started as Bala's trunk curled round her and lifted her. She found herself astride Bala's back, almost eye to eye with the trader. 'Come out of the pit! Leave the beast! Get down!' Carpus shouted, enraged.

From her new vantage point Aoife could see someone behind him: a hooded man, with his hands in chains. He looked up and she saw his face. It was Galen.

'What have you done!' Aoife cried.

'You were trying to trick me!' Carpus said. 'This man was heard giving orders to take the beast on to his ship! Come down! Leave the beast!' Seizing a firebrand in each hand, he stood at the edge of the slope.

Bala growled. Aoife held on tightly as the elephant threw back her head and roared. When Bala lowered her head, Carpus brought down his torches.

Bala reared as the brands burned the scar between the domes on her forehead. *'You! It was you!'* Aoife shouted, burning herself as she pushed the blazing reeds away from Bala's face. 'You burned her! You did it before, in Africa, when she was captured!'

'What if I did!' Carpus shouted. His guards dragged Aoife down from Bala's back, as Carpus took up more firebrands.

Before he could use them, Bala found purchase on the slope and, trumpeting with alarm, rushed up it. With a cry Carpus tried to jump back, but he stumbled, within reach of Bala's tusks.

With a light and easy gesture, she caught him up by his belt, swung him over the ground, then hurled him away, as if he were a rag tossed by the wind. Soldiers scattered from his path as he fell, fifty paces away.

'Ba-aala!' Aoife cried, escaping her guards as the elephant, held at bay by soldiers with firebrands, stamped at the edge of the pit.

In a quick movement, Bala turned and picked her up again, placing her securely on her back. A trumpet call sounded from the arena. 'Go! Attend the execution!' Aoife shouted to the soldiers, now surrounding her. 'You!' she said to the nearest guard. 'Attend Carpus Alexander.' The trumpet summoned them again and she shouted again to them all. 'Attend the execution. Leave me to calm the beast!'

No one moved and Aoife thought she was lost. Then a centurion lowered his firebrand and sent men to attend

Carpus Alexander. The men began to mutter and cast glances behind them, towards the arena, where a troupe of dancers was entertaining the crowd. Still guarded by a ring of soldiers with firebrands, Aoife could do nothing more. She did her best to calm Bala, with long strokes along the sides of her head and ears.

Soldiers took Carpus Alexander's body away. A group of green-cloaked traders appeared, to negotiate Galen's release. A pouch of coins changed hands: Galen's chains were removed. He and his traders moved away, in the direction of the horse pens. As he passed, Galen looked up at Aoife, but made no sign of knowing her.

There came a different call from the emperor's trumpets. Aoife looked towards the arena. From a path at right-angles to the main track, between the infirmary and prison tents, halfway down to the practice ground, Justinius staggered into view.

Bowed under the weight of a heavy wooden beam across his shoulders, he walked between two Praetorians who, with drawn swords, forced him down to the site of his execution.

Justinius. Aoife's spirit quailed. It was a show of puppets, not real people. It was not real: in her mind she fled to a distance until it seemed that she was watching Madoc and the other boys at home playing at executions.

'You!' The soldier's voice broke the memory. Aoife turned dull eyes on a captain, who had come with new orders. The guards lit fresh firebrands, to force Bala back into the pit. 'You! Get down from the beast!' he shouted. He spoke with authority, but shuffled hastily backwards as Bala lifted one of her front feet in his direction.

Rousing herself, Aoife looked for Galen. He was there, behind her, hurrying towards the horse pens.

A roar broke from the execution site. Justinius had fallen on his knees in front of the emperor. Aoife lost her breath. *Take me in his place. Let me die instead of Justinius.* 'You! The emperor's waiting!' She looked at the soldier, then back to the estuary path. *I have a chance to save Bala.* Commending Justinius to the Mother's care, she kicked Bala's sides, and the elephant set off, running, shoving guards and firebrands aside, as if she knew what she must do.

'NO-O-OOOO!' Aoife cried, tugging at Bala's ear. She was going the wrong way. With amazing speed, Bala charged down the track to the combat ground. It took all Aoife's strength to hold on as she thundered into the arena. With a curl of her trunk she snatched the upright timber of Justinius's cross from the ground, as if it were a sapling, and tossed it away. The soldiers guarding Justinius stumbled out of her path as Bala circled the prisoner. Claudius had leapt out of his seat. Now he stared past Bala to the other end of the camp, as the cry came: 'They're stealing the horses!'

A body of soldiers ran full pelt down the track to the animal pens. From atop Bala's back, Aoife could see what no one else could: the flames streaming from one of the barns, and cloaked figures driving the horses from the pens.

Three hundred horses, driven by men wielding smouldering branches, were in full stampede in every direction, away from the camp. Aoife thought she saw Galen, here, there, in many places, masterminding the whole operation.

As the call to arms was given, the spectators' benches emptied. Thinking the camp was under attack, the civilians, including the senators, hurried to save their possessions. The remaining soldiers hurried to the horse pens: only the Praetorians stayed with their emperor. Some stood around him; others, carrying spears, advanced on Bala.

Claudius signalled to the Praetorian who had been Justinius's deputy. The man drew his sword and, skirting the others, approached the prisoner, who was still on his knees, tied to his crossbeam. The other guards followed. Claudius was going to kill them all.

Aoife prompted Bala to protect Justinius. Under cover of a shower of spears, his deputy sprinted towards him. Bala reared and stamped to avoid the spears. The arena whirled around Aoife.

As a second wave of spears was hurled at them, she saw the Praetorian reach Justinius. He thrust his sword into his side.

Aoife screamed his name: *Justinius!* It was as if the sword had pierced her too. With a cry of surprise, the assassin fell back, arms wide, as a cloaked figure cut his throat. Wielding his bloody dagger, the man looked up at Aoife. 'For Edain!' he said. 'Aoife! Bevis's daughter! Rouse yourself!' A host of cloaked figures, the people of her tribe, fought with the guards surrounding the emperor. More followed, streaming out of the wood. As a spear zinged past her face, the man tugged at Aoife's tunic. 'My lady! You must leave this to us now. Go!'

They were carrying Justinius away. 'Go!' said the man. 'Take your beast! The ship's waiting!'

Her people were leaving the arena. As the last tribesman left the ground, Claudius called back his guards, countermanding the officer's order to pursue.

Aoife dug her heels into Bala's sides. The elephant crashed through the staked boundary fence as if it were brushwood.

Calm, now . . . calm . . . Aoife whispered, pressing her face and body on to Bala's bristly domed forehead, speaking as much to herself as to Bala, as they cantered into a landscape filled with mist. *Calm, now . . . calm . . . calm.*

Then, as she left the fury of fighting behind and entered the silent landscape of the marshes, as cold as death, a cry of grief broke from her; she could not prevent it. The pain of loss threatened to burst her body open. It shook her like a hound shaking its prey, and left her weak, so that she lay face down on Bala's back, her cheek pressed to the elephant's bristly hide.

Finally Bala's pace slackened, and, as Aoife breathed in the salt tang of the sea, friends came out of the mist to greet them. There were torches and voices, and arms reaching up to pat and stroke Bala and offer fresh grass and water and green apples. Someone clasped Aoife's hand.

She and Bala were guided to the edge of the marsh and on to the track leading down to the beach. There Bala stopped and, shivering, stood with her trunk lowered to the ground.

'Aoife.' Someone spoke to her. She raised her head and looked down into Galen's face.

LEAVE-TAKING

Word came that Claudius had dispatched a troop to recover the horses. They had further orders to kill the Celtish witch and her beast.

Aoife stroked Bala's side. She must take her to the ship. She could at least attempt to fulfil her vow. Laying her cheek to Bala's, she made another promise. *I'll find you again. One day I'll come to Africa and find the place with the red dust and the barn roofed with palm.* Bala moaned and stirred. *I will. I'll find you*, Aoife promised.

'Torches!' shouted the watchman. 'They're coming!'

'You're going home,' Aoife whispered. 'Safe journey. Live long.'

'We must leave,' Galen said urgently. Aoife reached for Bala's ear which lifted to her touch, then she prompted her on to the gangplank and into the ship.

'Send word when she has reached home safely,' Aoife said, handing Bala into the care of one of the traders. 'You'll send word?' she repeated, as the man led Bala down the ramp into the hold.

'He knows what to do.' Galen drew her away, as the ship's ropes were untied and thrown onto the deck.

As Aoife watched the ship move into the estuary, she

saw a movement at one of the portholes and the gleam of a small black eye.

'*Mother keep you,*' she whispered.

Shouts came again from the watchman, but Aoife stayed a while longer, listening to the sounds of Bala's leaving. The stroke of the oars and the wash of the tide strengthened her: in the matter of the elephant, she had defeated the emperor.

Roman trumpets sounded from the marsh.

'The times grind us between their stones,' Galen said. 'We are not yet masters of our fate. Until we are, you must put grief aside; it's your enemy.'

'I know it,' Aoife said. Her voice broke on the next words and she clenched her fists to stop them trembling as she forced herself to speak. 'From this hour, I am no longer the emperor's prisoner and elephant keeper. I am the daughter of Bevis, Caradoc's sister's child and, if Caradoc still needs me, I shall lead the tribe of Edain. I shall go to my people.' Galen smiled his approval. 'What will you do? Claudius will never trust you again, or your traders,' she went on. 'You have lost everything.'

'Daughter of Bevis, listen to me. We cannot fight them, so we must do all we can to survive, to gather strength for the fight to come, when the tribes will face them together. My men are, even now, rounding up the emperor's horses: I shall take them back to him.'

'*You'll be killed!*' Aoife said.

'No. Carpus is dead, so Claudius has no evidence that I was involved in releasing the horses. I may yet keep the trust of Rome.'

'Claudius knows that your ship carries his elephant! He knows that we are here together!'

'I shall tell him that you bewitched me, before vanishing like mist into the marsh. But not before I warn him about his lucky escape from the elephant, of how you had boasted of your plan to assassinate him during the procession, forcing the beast to throw him from its back on your signal.'

'*He won't believe such a tale! He's not a fool!*'

'No, he's not. But he will believe me when I produce the source of your power, your talisman.'

'*Talisman?*' She followed his gaze to the pouch on her belt.

Galen held out his hand.

'It's time to use it.' Aoife drew the pouch from her belt, unloosed it and took out the Mark of Edain.

'Do you really think this plan will work?' As she asked the question she could feel the answer growing like a seed inside her. *It will work. Listen to him.*

'Claudius will be pleased to see the back of the wild elephant. He has others to choose from for his procession, beasts far more docile. He will not take the trouble to pursue you into the west, when Caradoc himself is in retreat.'

'Galen—!' The watchman tumbled down the hill towards them.

The trader's horse shifted restlessly. 'Go to your people.'

Aoife pressed the Mark of Edain into his hand.

'Mother keep you,' she said.

Claudius's soldiers were everywhere. She had hoped to use the marsh mist to conceal her presence while she attempted to follow half-remembered paths, then, in a treacherous moment, when the fog lifted and exposed her like a lone wolf to the hunters, a score of men, with other ranks following them, closed in and cut off her escape.

They marched her back to the camp, where she saw Galen, with the lead horse from Claudius's stock roped to his own, rounding up the rest. He did not look at her.

When she was hauled into the emperor's presence, she stood alone.

'The sentence is death,' Claudius said, his voice sharp as a knife. 'I should have killed you in Rome, you and the beast. But I am merciful: there's no time for crucifixions. You will die in your own Celtish fashion. Take her to the so-called Well of Souls.'

THE WELL OF SOULS

They profaned the grove with their loud talk and laughter, their spitting and urinating on the stones. They made fun of the goddess's sigil, drawing obscene pictures around it or scratching it out with their knives.

They bound her and gagged her and made her wait, on her knees, next to the altar stone, until the emperor had finished the picnic he had brought to eat within the grove's precincts.

The Well of Souls. She hoped it would be a quick death; then, remembering, with a tremor of fear, the victim's cries she had heard as a child, she flushed for shame. She had no right to ask for a merciful end: that was cowardly and weak. She must be strong, as fearless in death as she would have tried to be in life, leading the tribe. She must not disgrace the name of Edain.

She thought of her nurse, Anwyn, who loved her as well as any mother; Anwyn, always singing, as Madoc sang, with such joy. She remembered a wedding, a joining of two families and a feast. She had fed a hound with her hog bones. *Ban*. Where was he now?

She remembered the brand on the hound's neck, the mark of the tribe, and thought of her own branding, and the sting of the thorn as her father had pricked it into her skin, then the glory of Anwyn's voice, singing the praise of Edain, afterwards. '*Is it over?*' she had asked and Bevis had smiled and said: '*Almost . . .* ' then dipped the thorn into the dye again, to make the three lines of his own mark. '*It's over,*' he said.

'Take her to the pit!' Harsh hands dragged her to her feet and bundled her through the entrance into the inner grove. They were all silent now: cold, efficient, brutal conquerors. Soldiers mounted a guard: in equal numbers, some faced the pit, some the wood. Claudius entered the inner grove. The soldier's torches flared as he passed, as if in a gust of wind.

'Remove her gag! Stand her up on the ledge!' he ordered. The greasy cloth was snatched from her mouth: Aoife swallowed; her mouth was dry. Her feet and hands were still bound. On the narrow wall surrounding the pit, it was difficult to keep her balance.

'Have you anything to say, Celt, before you join your ancestors?'

Aoife stood up straight and still. She looked over the heads of the soldiers, into the trees.

'Tell my story,' she said, 'and the story of all those who resist the might of Rome. Tell the truth of how you conquered me and my people.'

Claudius raised his hand to give the signal. The guard standing behind Aoife readied himself.

She looked down into the pit.

'*Mother! Edain! I commit myself to your care—*' she said, then, before Claudius could give the signal, with her eyes wide open, she leaped into the Well of Souls.

* * *

She was not dead. During the fall she had closed her eyes, on instinct, as earth and leaves showered around her. When she opened them again, she was lying on a springy bed of straw that pricked her cheeks, telling her she was still alive. She looked up at the circle of starlit sky far above. There were no soldiers there. She pricked her ears and listened, but there was no sound of the emperor's guards. How long since she had leaped into the well? How long had she been here?

Her head thumped with pain. She must have lost time, lying, unconscious, after the fall. She rolled off the bed of straw and on to hard dry ground. A badly winded body, but no broken bones.

She was still bound, but the ties had worked loose and it was the work of moments to free herself. She stood up and felt her way around the walls of the pit. There was no way out. The walls were dry but smooth, impossible to climb. She clambered back on to the springy bed, to see how far she could reach, feeling with outstretched fingers for some kind of handhold. There was none. She jumped down again and sat with her back to the wall, looking up at the round full moon, which now shone into the well.

There was no sound. Her enemies were long gone. She sighed and shifted her aching legs, then froze. There was the thump of footsteps, the low murmur of voices. She could not tell where the sounds came from. Perhaps she was dead after all. Her heart beat fast at the idea of spirits coming to fetch her and take her into their realm. She was not dead! They must not take her!

Inch by inch, her fingers crept over the cold wall of the well and touched the edge of a mat of woven creepers. Woven, twisted together with a defined warp and weft, by human hands, not spirits'. She dragged at the mat and it fell from the wall. Behind it was the narrow opening into a tunnel. Yes! Of course! This was the way into the well, used by the men of the tribe to remove the bodies of those thrown into it.

She had peered into the well as a child, fascinated, full of a compulsion of horror at the thought of seeing the broken body of the felon. The well had been empty. There was no one there. Dimock said that the goddess removed the corpses, but she had wondered how he had acquired an elaborate gold cuff, which, spying once, unseen, on the ritual, she had noticed on the wrist of a felon as he was pushed into the well. That question was now answered.

There was just room to push herself inside the tunnel. Crouching she followed it, for thirty paces, then it began to rise. She gasped as the air grew colder. There were faint pinpricks of starlight ahead.

She emerged into the forest. There was a grey horse, tied to a tree, with a skin of fresh water and a sack of food. Someone had expected her to survive her leap into the well. They had known she would find the tunnel. She untied the horse and mounted. He set off, without her prompting, down the long track to the west.

EPILOGUE

She rode into Caradoc's stronghold, past his guards and straight into his presence. Smiling faces. Welcoming hands. Home-coming.

Aoife sprang from her horse and went to greet her king, the rebel leader of all Britannia, to whom she must pledge the loyalty and strength of her tribe. Placing her open hand, palm down, on her chest, she bowed to the man who sat at ease on his high chair on the dais.

'Daughter of Bevis—' he said.

'Lord Caradoc,' Aoife replied. His face was lined, worn old with grief.

'I'm sorry for the death of your brother, Togodumnus,' she said, surprised that she spoke so quietly, stumbling over the words, finding that she could not easily speak of death.

She lost her words altogether when Caradoc replied, in the same quiet tone: 'You too have lost a brother. I am sorry for it. There have been too many deaths.'

Pushing grief aside, she lifted her face to look at him boldly. Here, she was not only Aoife, Bevis's last surviving child; she was now the leader of the tribe of Edain.

'My lord, I am here to place my sword at your disposal, and the swords of my tribe—' Her pledge was interrupted by the arrival of a young girl, armed for battle, who strode confidently into the hall.

'You may remember Boudicca of the Iceni,' he said, gesturing to the young girl at his side. 'Like you, she dreams of freedom.'

The girl was smaller and younger than Aoife, who thought she remembered this Boudicca as a child of four or five years, climbing trees with the rest and causing alarm when she sat on the top branch and refused to come down.

Boudicca's spear thudded to the ground. 'Hail, Caradoc!' she said, in her young girl's voice. Her hair stood up around her head like flames. She looked at Aoife. 'Today we lie in wait,' she said. 'But the day will come when almighty Rome will feel our strength. Until then—' she touched the tip of her finger to the tip of her spear—'we shall be like wasps: those who try to trap us shall feel our sting!' She grinned at Aoife, who returned a wan smile. What did this child know of the Romans?

Caradoc glanced up as someone entered the hall. With her back to the door, Aoife did not see who it was at first. 'Aoife,' said Caradoc. 'Your sister welcomes you, Aoife!'

Igren. She swung round. 'Igren!' She hugged her close, marvelling that she was real. So tall, so strong: her sister was a warrior. Edain had saved her: golden Igren.

'Thank the Mother you're alive!' Igren said.

'And you!' breathed Aoife, her face pressed to Igren's hard shoulder.

In the shadows, someone else waited to greet her. Someone who began to sing the home song, the sound touching her as lightly as the brush of a moth's wing, yet taking her strength away, just as it had when Madoc had sung to her in the streets of Rome. *Madoc.*

This was not her brother. Confused, she dared not look round. The voice was deeper, richer, of someone older. She listened to the song, hardly daring to hope.

'Where salt sea flows, where wild herb grows,
Where hawk flies free, and curlew calls
Where flint strikes flame
Home, hearth, and fire—'

When the song was done, Caradoc spoke.

'Welcome, Huw, son of Erian.'

The shock pricked through Aoife's body.

'Justinius!' she cried. 'Justinius!' She left Igren, she forgot Lord Caradoc and his court, and she ran to him, the one who stepped out of the shadows to meet her. She stopped short of embracing him: Justinius stood, pale, with the wound in his chest tightly bound. Solemn, she studied his face, lined, weary, yet with a hoard of stories to tell.

'You're here at last,' he said. 'You've come home.'

She moved. She stepped forward. 'Well?' he said, and held out his arms.

AUTHOR'S NOTE

The Roman Emperor Claudius came to Britain in AD 43, bringing elephants, shortly after his legions had defeated the British rebels in the south-east. No one knows how the elephants were brought to Britain, nor how they were traded or kept. The ways of controlling such large animals, by ham-stringing them—cutting the large tendon on one of the back legs—and the use of tools to slaughter them if they got out of hand, are both documented.

So many people helped me with *The Mark of Edain*: the Scottish mystic who told me I would have been a Celt in Roman times; the bookshop owner who gave me the correct name for the British leader—*Carat*acus, not *Caract*acus; the librarian at Colchester, who found me the evidence for Roman elephants in Essex.

Special thanks to Andy Durham of Whipsnade Zoological Society of London, and his elephant, Karishma, who trotted across the field to take a close look at me when I arrived.

Once I'd met Karishma, the urge to write the story of Aoife and Bala was irresistible.

Pauline Chandler 2008

PAULINE CHANDLER

Pauline Chandler was born in Nottinghamshire. After student years in London, she became a teacher and now teaches children with special needs. Pauline began to write seriously during a year's break in Cornwall. Her first short stories were published in local and national magazines. Besides writing, she enjoys gardens, wild woods, cats and architecture. Pauline lives with her family in a former Victorian gasworks in Derbyshire. *The Mark of Edain* is her third novel for Oxford University Press.

If you enjoyed The Mark of Edain, you'll love **Warrior Girl,**
also by Pauline Chandler.
Here is a special extract, from the first chapter . . .

MARIANE

It was my grandmother who saved me. I was making everyone sick with my screams, the wordless noise that said *I want my mother! I want my mother!* They were all pleading with me to stop, but I couldn't help myself. Like a hog driven to slaughter, I bit and kicked and scratched. I stuck my foot in the door of my mother's room as they tried to push me away, dug my nails into the wood of the jambs until the ends of my fingers bled, all the time making animal grunts, my eyes forever fixed on the smudge of blood, that wrongness, at the side of my mother's mouth.

Through the closing gap of the doorway I saw my aunts arranging her body, one of them wiping the blood away, as my grandmother's arms closed on mine. Her arms are as strong as steel and brook no argument. So, as she prised me away, I gave in to her, let her lead me downstairs, let her sit me on her lap as if I were a baby again. And she held me so tight that, in the end, my rage vanished and I clung to her, because I knew she was saving my life.

My mother's murderers would have cut me down too if I'd run after them. And I would have, make no mistake; I would have dashed after them straight into hell itself, to kill or to be killed, but for my grandmother.

Even though I am grown, almost ready to marry and leave home, I submitted to the treatment: for hours she wrapped her shawl around me, and held me tight, rocking my heartache, singing. I think she expected, or, in the end, hoped, that it would bring back my voice.

Grandmère had a repertoire of songs which she sang to me during this time, always in the same order, one after the other, until I was soothed into sleep. My favourite was the first: '*Viens par le pré, ma belle*', 'Come into the meadow, my pretty girl'—as I sing it again, silently in my head, I can feel grandmère's warm breath on my face and hear again the soft sound of her voice as she murmured the words. The song is imprinted on my mind like a map to tell me who I am and where I've come from. One day, I'm going home, that's my plan: when the time's right, I'll go back there, I'll just go. Of course, Uncle Jacques will try to stop me.

I was sent here because it's too dangerous for me in Reims. Well, I shan't tell him: I'll wait until he's away or busy with the harvest or until I think he's forgotten my existence, then I'll grab my bag and I'll go home. I won't let grandmère send me back again.

They say it's a long dangerous road from Domrémy to Reims, but I'll travel at night, using the ditches and tracks that no one else uses. I'll stay off the road: the English are all over it like a rash. Even if I were seen, no one would bother with me. I'm a 'throwback', according to Uncle Jacques, a dimblebat, an idiot, because I can't speak. It makes me angry, but I don't let on. Underneath I'm stoking my rage, turning it into the energy I need to get back to Reims.

It's hot today, hot September. This field of turnips looks small from the farmhouse, but when you're in it and not even halfway through pulling the crop, it stretches out to infinity. To be honest, I couldn't care less if I never see another turnip in my life. I've been doing this job all week, with my cousin Jehanne. Which means, more or less, by myself, because as soon as Jehanne has filled her quota of baskets, which she does at top speed, she's off into Long Meadow. She lies down in the stubble, prostrate, like a nun in a church, making the sign of the cross with her body on the ground and she lies like that, quite silent, for hours. She says she is attending to God. She says she is listening for His message. This seems devout, but it can't be right, can it?

I hate turnips. They don't even taste nice. These are purple. Last week we pulled the yellow. The leaves are so hairy and rough, turnip-pulling ruins your hands. I wish my hands were like those of Father Cornelius: his hands are as soft as lamb's wool and his eyes are deep, like brown pools on a hot summer's day. I'd like my husband to look like Father Cornelius. He's slim and strong and his face goes quite still when he looks at you, which makes you feel special. The only thing is that sometimes a cold look comes in his eyes, as if he knows all your sins and has got you signed, sealed, judged, and sent to damnation.

He'd better not find out about Jehanne lying down in the fields. He'd probably think she was showing off and getting above her station; a mere woman trying to listen to God by herself instead of in church at the proper time. He wouldn't like that, I know he wouldn't. But if he asked me about her, I couldn't lie, so he'd better not.

She's getting to her feet. I shade my eyes to get a better view. She always knows when it's time for the bells to ring out the call to prayer and she stands facing the church, listening, as if the bells are ringing just for her.

'Mariane! Mariane!' It's Jehanne's mother, my aunt Isabeau. She's standing by the gate into the farmyard, tying a scarf round her hair. 'Where's Jehanne?'

Something's happened. She never fetches us from the fields, but she's hitched up her skirt and is treading over the ruts in the lane, crossing over to the gate. She stops and shades her eyes.

'Mariane!' I wave to show that I've heard, push floppy strands of damp hair back under my headscarf and rub the sweat from my brow, ready to pay attention. 'Where's Jehanne? I need you both back at the house.'

As if I've not heard the question, I wave again and walk down the field towards her, carrying two baskets of turnips, one in each hand.

'Where's Jehanne?' she says again.

As I get close to her, I stumble and spill my load at her feet. There are small dusty turnips rolling in every direction. Some end up in a stinking puddle, causing a cloud of shiny blue and green flies to explode into the air.

'Oh God—' she says, batting the flies away from her face, '—never mind—oh, dear—are you all right, Mariane—oh dear—never mind—' Automatically she helps me re-load the baskets, her mind obviously elsewhere.

'I'll take these,' she says finally, stowing the load under her arms. Then she says sharply, 'Fetch Jehanne. I need you both now.' As she turns away I hear her speaking to herself under her breath, as if organizing the tasks in her mind. 'We can use the dog-cart. One of them can pull it with a shoulder harness. Pray God it doesn't rain,' and then she's gone.

I climb back to where I can see Jahanne standing in the middle of the meadow, as still as a rock. Everything around her is still; the long grass, the poppies, the flax, stand as if in a painting. The insects are still and the birds. The trees look as if they're listening, or waiting, or both.

As I walk towards her I try not to make a sound, because I don't want to break the silence. Jehanne's silence. It's as if she can stop the world. I don't know how she does it, but I can feel it.

As I get close she turns slightly to look at me with that special smile of hers and the silence is broken and all the world moves again. I hear the hum of bees and the swish of the wind through the trees. As Jehanne steps forward to meet me a skylark rises from the ground at her feet. We both stop and tilt our heads, watching it soar high into the wide blue sky . . .